For more than forty years,
Yearling has been the leading name
in classic and award-winning literature
for young readers.

Yearling books feature children's
favorite authors and characters,
providing dynamic stories of adventure,
humor, history, mystery, and fantasy.

Trust Yearling paperbacks to entertain,
inspire, and promote the love of reading
in all children.

DRAGON KEEPERS

DRAGON KEEPERS 🐉 BOOK 2

THE DRAGON
IN THE
DRIVEWAY

KATE KLIMO

with illustrations
by
JOHN SHROADES

A Yearling Book

For Ethan,
who super-duper wanted another book

Text copyright © 2009 by Kate Klimo
Illustrations copyright © 2009 by John Shroades

All rights reserved. Published in the United States by Yearling, an imprint of Random House Children's Books, a division of Random House, Inc., New York. Originally published in hardcover in the United States by Random House Children's Books, a division of Random House, Inc., New York, in 2009.

Yearling and the jumping horse design are registered trademarks of Random House, Inc.

Visit us on the Web! www.randomhouse.com/kids

Educators and librarians, for a variety of teaching tools, visit us at www.randomhouse.com/teachers

www.foundadragon.org

The Library of Congress has cataloged the hardcover edition of this work as follows:
Klimo, Kate.
The dragon in the driveway / Kate Klimo ; with illustrations by John Shroades.
p. cm. — (Dragon keepers ; bk. 2)
Summary: Cousins Jesse and Daisy, along with their pet dragon, continue their battle against the evil scientist who has plans to destroy the forest in order to find the magical golden ax that is buried there.
ISBN 978-0-375-85589-4 (trade) — ISBN 978-0-375-95589-1 (lib. bdg.) — ISBN 978-0-375-89293-6 (e-book)
[1. Dragons—Fiction. 2. Magic—Fiction. 3. Cousins—Fiction.] I. Shroades, John, ill. II. Title.
PZ7.K67896Dp 2009
[Fic]—dc22
2008034050

ISBN 978-0-375-85590-0 (pbk.)

Printed in the United States of America

10 9 8 7 6 5 4 3 2 1

First Yearling Edition

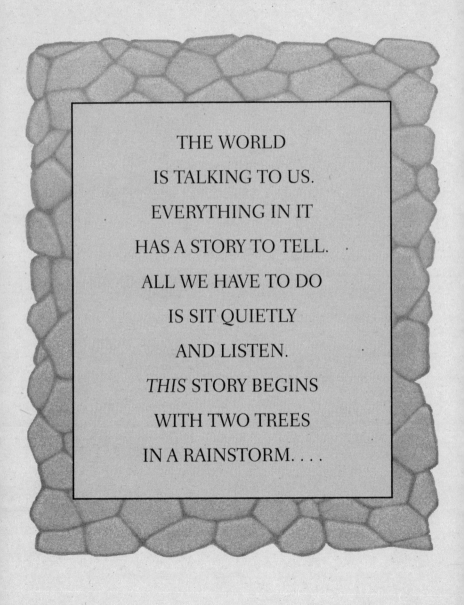

THE WORLD
IS TALKING TO US.
EVERYTHING IN IT
HAS A STORY TO TELL.
ALL WE HAVE TO DO
IS SIT QUIETLY
AND LISTEN.
THIS STORY BEGINS
WITH TWO TREES
IN A RAINSTORM. . . .

CONTENTS

CHAPTER ONE

AN ILL WIND

Dear Mom and Dad, It is still raining. The local weather guy says it's a record. Not as bad as India that time the Jeep floated away, but pretty bad. Our dog, Emmy, got tired of being cooped up in the garage. She got out

and ran down the driveway into the street.
Aunt Maggie went nuts! She made these
poor guys come in the rain and put in an
invisible fence. It's this underground wire
that is supposed to keep the dog in the yard.
One step over it and whammo, she really
gets zapped. (Don't tell Aunt Maggie, but
Emmy runs right over it anyway!)

Ten-year-old Jesse reread his e-mail. He hadn't
included the information that the dog had turned
back into a dragon for an instant the first time
she was zapped, and that Mrs. Nosy-Britches, who
lived across the street, was standing at her mailbox
at the exact moment the zap happened.

"It's the oddest thing," Mrs. Nosy-Britches kept
saying to anyone who would listen, "but I could
swear I saw this very large lizard in the driveway
across the street. If I didn't know better, I'd swear it
was some sort of a *dragon*."

Jesse finished and sent the e-mail. He listened
to the rain rattling on the roof and watched the
slide show on the screen saver. The pictures were
of him and his parents in some of the places where
they had traveled and lived. Looking at it made him
happy, if a little homesick for his parents and even
the places: India, Africa, Costa Rica. . . . When he

had first come to America to stay with his cousin Daisy, who was also ten, he had been so homesick that he had worn two wristwatches, one showing the time in the U.S. and the other the time in Africa, where his parents were. These days he wore just the one watch showing American time, but when there wasn't quite enough to keep him busy, like now, he missed his parents.

Jesse was just shutting down the computer when he heard Daisy scream out his name. He leaped up, tore downstairs, slid down the hall in his socks, and collided with the kitchen table.

"What?" he said, panting. "What is it, Daze?"

Daisy was standing on a footstool gazing out the window over the sink. Her long white-blond hair was tucked behind her ears, which were pointy like an elf's and bright pink with excitement.

"Jess, *look!*" she said, tapping the windowpane.

Jesse looked, but the panes were fogging up from Daisy's breath. "What are we looking at?" he asked.

"Don't you *see?*" Daisy whispered. "There and *there?*"

Jesse boosted himself up onto the edge of the sink, leaned over, and rubbed a clear spot in the bottom pane. He stared hard through the porthole into the side yard. Trunks and leaves and branches were all churned up into one great green swarming, sopping mess.

"Boy, oh, boy," he said, mustering some appreciation for the view. "The wind sure is blowing hard."

Daisy tugged impatiently at the hood of his sweatshirt. "The two trees, Jess. See them?"

"*Which* two trees?" he said.

She groaned. "Get down and let me look."

They switched places. Daisy pointed and said, "They're standing right there, exactly ten feet from the house. I swear, Jess, those trees were not there before."

Jesse shivered. "How can you tell?" he asked.

"Simple. There isn't either a Douglas fir or a quaking aspen growing in our side yard," Daisy said, getting down from the sink. "Plus they both have a bright strip of cloth or ribbon or something wrapped around their trunks. You can't miss them."

Even though he had been living in Daisy's house for nearly six months, Jesse didn't know every tree in the yard. That was Daisy's thing. Her favorite saying was "Not knowing the names of the flowers and the trees is like not knowing the names of your own sisters and brothers."

Jesse craned his neck and gave the side yard another scan. He couldn't see anything out of place or any bright strips of cloth. He didn't want to make Daisy feel bad, but he didn't want to lie just to make her feel good. "Sorry, Daze. I just don't see what you're seeing."

Daisy's face turned bright pink to match her ears. Before Jesse could say another word, she ran out of the kitchen. He heard her stocking feet pounding up the stairs. Seconds later, she slammed her bedroom door so hard, he flinched and drew the hood of his sweatshirt up. He took one last glance out the window just as a gust of wind came up and bent the trees toward the house, wagging their branches at him like long scolding fingers.

Jesse sighed. "I didn't say I didn't *believe* her," he explained to the trees, as if they were the members of a jury. "I just said I didn't see it myself."

Suddenly the wind let up for a moment and the trees straightened. They looked stern but satisfied.

This storm is making us all wacky, Jesse thought. Cabin fever: that was what Aunt Maggie had called it that morning before she left for work at the ad company. It did feel as if they were trapped in the cabin of a ship that was riding out an endless storm. It had been raining for five days. How much longer could it go on?

Jesse grabbed a container of coleslaw from the refrigerator and headed for the mudroom. Dragon

7

Keepers didn't get time off, even in bad weather, and Emmy would be hungry for her midmorning snack of something rich in calcium. He pulled on his yellow rain poncho, still damp from the morning, when he had delivered Emmy her breakfast of leftover Brussels sprouts au gratin with a side of dandelion greens.

Jesse pulled up the poncho hood and opened the back door. The rain hit him full in the face. He stepped back into the shelter of the doorway and peered around. Leaves and broken branches lay everywhere. In the backyard, the light shone in the Rock Shop, the garden shed his uncle Joe had converted into a lab for his geology studies. Uncle Joe was hard at work on a project.

Jesse took a deep breath and plunged off the back landing, down the steps, and into the swirling wetness. The rain blinded him, so he followed his feet over the leaf-strewn ground to the garage. He groped around in his pocket for the key and fit it into the lock. Then he flung open the side door and kicked it shut, leaning against it to catch his breath.

"Jesse!" said the dragon, beside herself with joy at the sight of him. She bounded over, her long green tail smacking the concrete floor.

"Jesse—Jesse—Jesse!" Emmy had been able to speak since the minute she hatched. The sound of her voice still gave Jesse a thrill. It was one of a kind—rich and rippling, like molten gold.

Jesse raised his voice over the rain drumming loudly on the garage's steel roof. "I brought you a snack!" He showed her the coleslaw.

Emmy shook her head and pulled back. "No cabbage swill for me now, please, thank you. Aunt Maggie says I have robin fever," she told him.

Jesse laughed. "That's *cabin* fever, Em. And I'm afraid I don't have a cure for it," he said.

"Going outside will make me alllllll better," Emmy said coyly. "Now? Please? Thank you. You're welcome." She swirled gracefully in a blue-green spiral and then drifted to a standstill before him.

Although she had been no bigger than a kitten when she had hatched four weeks before, now she was as big as a pony. There were two bumps on her shoulder blades, which Jesse thought might turn into wings. Two dark ridges ran down Emmy's back and along her tail. A single horn sprouted from her head, which was shaped like a sea horse's, only broader. She still smelled faintly of chili peppers, although the scent was fading as fast as her baby talk. Emmy's eyes were large and sparkly and as green as emeralds. It had been her eyes that had inspired Jesse to name her Emerald. Those eyes looked a little sad now as she settled down with her tail curled around her, like a great green cat, and said, "Why is our Daisy Flower unhappy today?"

Jesse shot Emmy a curious look. "How do you know Daisy's unhappy?" he asked. "And since when is she Daisy *Flower*?"

"Since I say so. She is Daisy Flower, just like you are Jesse Tiger," Emmy said.

"Don't remind me," he groaned. Tiger was his middle name, but sometimes he would just as soon forget.

"Why is she sad?" Emmy asked.

Jesse shrugged. "She saw something and I didn't see it and she got upset."

Emmy cocked her head. "Daisy has a cabin fever, too," she said. "Daisy will go outside, just like Emmy. Then our cabins will cool down!"

Jesse chuckled. "Well, I'm not sure how much better you're going to feel playing in the storm," he told her.

"Not playing," said Emmy. She added with a sly hiss, "S-s-spying."

"Spying?" Jesse asked.

"Spying on the Dragon Slayer," Emmy said with a knowing nod.

That would be a switch. It was usually St. George who spied on *them*, wanting to find Emmy. Every day for two weeks he had parked his big black Cadillac outside their house, from nine to five, like it was his job. If Jesse and Daisy went out, he followed. Jesse nearly laughed, thinking about it. St. George had hardly been stealthy about his spying! Then he had disappeared with the rain, as abruptly as the sunshine and the blue sky.

"The bad man has a bad plan!" Emmy said. "We will spy on him in his den. Then we will steal his big book!"

St. George's "den" was a lab in the zoology department of the Goldmine City College of Mining and Science, where he was posing as a herpetologist, or reptile scientist. In the first week of Emmy's life, St. George had stolen Emmy from the cousins. The cousins had gone to his den and stolen her back. That was when they had seen the big book. It was as big as a door and as thick as five phone books. The cover was too heavy to lift and the gold writing cut into the dark red leather was in a language neither of the cousins had ever seen.

"Spying! Brilliant," said Jesse. "That ought to cheer up Daisy. I'll go tell her. You eat the cabbage swill."

Emmy took the container in her agile forepaws. "I will eat it allllll up . . . for Jesse Tiger! Thank you, please."

"You're welcome, please, Emmy Dragon," said

Jesse. Then he ran back to the house, careful as always to lock the door behind him. When he passed through the mudroom into the kitchen, he was surprised to find Daisy back up on the edge of the sink, her nose pressed to the windowpane again.

"They're gone, Jess," she said in a small, forlorn voice. "Those two trees with the strips of cloth wrapped around their trunks I said I saw? They're gone."

"Really?" Jesse said. From where he was standing, it all looked the same. Still, he was sorry that the trees had gone before he had gotten a chance to try to look for them again.

"Maybe they were never there in the first place," Daisy said sadly. She jumped down from the sink and hugged herself hard. "Maybe this was one of those times when I wanted to believe the magic so badly, I saw what I wanted to see, rather than what was really there."

"Or maybe," Jesse said gently, "the trees had to go someplace else and they'll come back later . . . when they're ready to show themselves to both of us."

The corners of Daisy's lips turned up a fraction. "Then you believe me?"

"Hey," he said, "two months ago, if somebody had told me that we'd have a dragon living in our garage, I would have said they were wacky. Now . . . who knows what can happen, right?"

Daisy nodded, but she still seemed a little down, so Jesse told her about Emmy's plan.

Daisy perked up right away. "I'll tell my pops we're going over to the college to see the documentary they're showing on global climate change. Boy, is that ever appropriate," she said, cocking a thumb at the window. "You turn off the invisible fence. We wouldn't want to give Mrs. Nosy-Britches another flash of dragon."

Jesse went down to the basement circuit breaker and flipped the switch that controlled the invisible fence, and then, still in his poncho, he returned to the garage. Emmy was just licking the coleslaw container with her long pink forked tongue when Daisy burst through the door and slammed it behind her. She had a big scowl on her face. "Pops says we can't go out gallivanting—not until the rain stops," she said.

Jesse groaned, but Emmy asked eagerly, "When the rain stops piddling down, *then* we can go out?"

"That's what the rock doc said," Daisy replied gloomily, plopping down onto an old picnic bench.

"Yeah, but who knows when *that*'ll be?" Jesse added, plopping down next to her.

"I do!" said Emmy, her irises beginning to spin

like a set of brilliant green pinwheels. Her nostrils gave off three puffs of peppery pinkish smoke, which rose up and radiated outward, filling the entire garage with a bright, hot, pulsing light.

The next instant, the rain stopped drumming on the roof.

CHAPTER TWO

THE TREE SLAYER

"Now?" said Emmy, nodding brightly at the cousins. "We go out gallivanting now, please? Thank you, you're welcome, don't mention it. *My pleasure!*"

"Holy moly!" said Daisy.

"How did you *do* that?" Jesse asked the dragon.

"Weather spell," said Emmy, looking very pleased with herself.

"Yes, but who taught you?" Jesse asked.

"The book taught me," Emmy said.

"The big book?" Jesse asked.

Emmy nodded eagerly.

Jesse looked around, as if the big book might be in the garage. "Where is it?"

Emmy shrugged. "Somewhere nearby, I think. I want it. I need it. It's MINE!"

Jesse and Daisy both stared at the dragon with wide eyes.

"The big book is yours?" Daisy asked.

"Maybe," said Emmy. "Perhaps. Possibly. Don't know. Yes."

"What are we waiting for, then?" Daisy said. With that, she leaped up, ran to the side door, and flung it open.

Jesse followed her. They poked their heads out. The trees were still dripping, but not a drop more came down from the sky, and the wind was now a gentle breeze. A bright blue crack suddenly opened in the clouds, and a sunbeam struck the back lawn like a spotlight. Steam, smelling of crushed flowers and wet dirt, rose up from the earth.

Jesse grinned at Daisy. "Too bad we didn't ask

for this five days ago," he said. "Well . . . what are we waiting for?"

"It's time to spy!" Daisy said as the cousins shucked their ponchos and launched into their own private celebration jig, which they called the happy prospector's dance.

Daisy danced over to Emmy. "Leash time for you, young lady," she said.

Emmy pulled back with a disgusted little snort. "That leash stinks like dragon piddle," she said.

"Stinky or not," Jesse said, "Aunt Maggie says no leash, no walk. And what have we said about Aunt Maggie?"

Emmy heaved a dreary sigh. "Aunt Maggie is the boss."

"Exactly!" said Daisy. She clipped the leash onto Emmy's bright purple Great Dane–size invisible fence collar, to which Daisy had also attached the gold baby locket her mother had passed down to her. The gold in the locket fortified the growing dragon, like vitamins. Plus, Emmy was very fond of it because it contained two miniature photographs of her Keepers—Jesse and Daisy.

Jesse unlocked and rolled up the big folding garage door.

If Mrs. Nosy-Britches had peered out from

behind her living room curtain, she would have seen two kids walking an English sheepdog on a leash. That was because Emmy was using a masking spell. Masking is a power that dragons use to hide by assuming the appearance of another animal. Such was the power of Emmy's spell that everyone who saw her at these times, even Jesse and Daisy, sensed, felt, heard, and even *smelled* nothing but one hundred percent sheepdog. And it was a mighty good thing that while her dragon self kept growing, her sheepdog body remained the same size.

Daisy ran to the Rock Shop and told her father they were leaving now that the rain had stopped. Then they set off for the college on foot because the wet leaves made it too slippery to ride their bikes.

At the corner of their dead-end street, they stopped at Miss Alodie's little stone house with the blue shutters. Miss Alodie herself was outside, clad in a shiny bright green slicker, cleaning up the mess the storm had made in her garden. Miss Alodie's daisies were bigger than sunflowers, her sunflowers were bigger than fruit trees, and her tea roses were as big as Frisbees.

Miss Alodie made soothing noises as she snipped off the broken leaves and splinted the cracked stems of her rosebushes. Pink and white and yellow and red petals carpeted the ground at her feet like confetti.

Daisy tugged at Jesse's sleeve and pointed. "Look," she whispered.

Jesse nodded thoughtfully. A new fence, low to the ground and fashioned from sticks and string, now surrounded Miss Alodie's picture-perfect garden. Knotted around the string, every three feet or so, was a scrap of bright fabric with a flowered pattern.

"There, there, my loves, perk up, now," Jesse and Daisy heard Miss Alodie murmur. "It's not so bad, is it? Mother will have you back in the pink soon enough. Pan's pipes, but that man's wrought a world of woe, hasn't he, now?"

"Hey, Miss Alodie!" Daisy called out.

Miss Alodie looked up, her face alight at the sight of them. "Heigh-ho, cousins!" she called out.

"What's the new fence for?" Daisy asked.

"Is it to keep out pests?" Jesse asked.

Miss Alodie's sparkling blue eyes turned steely. "Something like that," she said. Then she saw Emmy and beamed again. "If it isn't my very favorite canine cohort!" she said. Emmy barked once and sat up, offering her right paw over the top of the fence. "Aren't you the clever boots?" she said, giving Emmy's paw a smart little shake.

"She can fetch and beg, too," said Jesse.

This was no time to show off Emmy's tricks. Daisy took Jesse's hand and tugged him and Emmy's leash with equal urgency. "Have a great day, Miss Alodie. We'll be seeing you."

As soon as they had gone around the corner, Daisy stopped Jesse and whipped him around to face her. "That flowered material on the fence, Jess!" she said.

"It looks like she tore up one of her old shirts," said Jesse. "What about it?"

Daisy moved in closer. "It's *exactly* like the strips of cloth I saw tied around the trunks of those two trees," she said.

Jesse's eyes went wide. "Really? Maybe we should go back and ask her about it."

Daisy shook her head. "Let's ask on the way home. We're on a mission, right?"

"Right," said Jesse, his eyes narrowing. "A spying mission."

"So let's do it!" she said. As they walked across town to the college, Daisy stared suspiciously at the trees. Many had lost branches and at least half of their summer growth of leaves, which lay in a thick sodden carpet beneath their feet. Emmy kept slurping up huge mouthfuls of wet leaves. For her it was an eight-block-long, all-you-can-eat salad bar.

When they reached the college parking lot, they saw very few cars, and St. George's big black Cadillac wasn't there, for sure. They raced across campus to the zoology building, where they dived into the wet bushes and crawled through the muck to peek in the basement windows. All the lab windows were closed, and St. George had rigged a curtain of sheets over them to discourage prying eyes. But Daisy went to the window they knew had a broken latch and pushed it gently. It swung open. Daisy snaked a couple of fingers in and tried to lift the sheet, but she couldn't reach it.

"I need a stick or something," she whispered to Jesse.

"Right," Jesse whispered back. He crawled around in the wet bushes, searching for a stick long enough to reach the sheet. He had just found a good one when a man came around the corner wearing the green uniform of a campus guard. Jesse froze until the guard had walked away. Then he crawled back to Daisy with the stick.

Daisy took the stick and poked it carefully through the gap in the window, moving aside the sheet just enough to offer them a look inside the lab. Jesse, Daisy, and Emmy leaned forward, cheek to cheek to cheek, and peered under the sheet into St. George's lab.

"Huh?" Jesse said.

"What?" Daisy said. She shoved the window wide open and snatched the sheet aside.

Jesse sat back on his heels. Emmy crouched down and started barking shrilly.

"Easy, Em," said Jesse, grabbing hold of her collar. But he didn't blame her for being upset. He felt the same way.

The mounds of geodes, the thunder eggs, were gone. The table saw that St. George had used to cut them open was gone. The hot plates, microwaves, and freezing chambers were gone. And most important of all, the big book was gone, too.

"Where did he go?" Jesse said. He had dreaded laying eyes on St. George again, but *not* seeing him—and not knowing where he was—made Jesse far more uneasy.

Emmy began to whimper.

"It's okay, Emmy. Everything's going to be fine," Jesse murmured, wishing he believed that himself.

"Maybe someone here knows where he went," Daisy said.

So they all backed out of the bushes and went in search of someone who might know St. George's whereabouts. Finally, they tracked down a man from the campus police, who told them that the reptile man had "flown the coop" the week before without leaving a forwarding address.

Daisy turned to Jesse and said gravely, "We need to report this to Professor Andersson."

Jesse nodded. Professor Andersson was their online consultant on all matters concerning dragons. Just after Emmy had hatched from the thunder egg, they had been lucky enough to stumble onto his site. "Let's go," said Jesse.

Jesse and Daisy tried to hurry home, but Emmy stopped every few blocks and wouldn't budge until they had smothered her with hugs and kisses and reassurances that everything would be all right. When the cousins had finally pulled down the garage door and unfastened her leash, Emmy shivered and shook, droplets of moisture spinning off her in a fine spray. Jesse and Daisy watched as the blur of white gradually turned to blue-green. When Emmy stopped, wet dog had become dry dragon in mere seconds.

"I'm a scaredy-dragon," Emmy told them. "A scaredy-dragon needs a cozy nest of socks, please." She crept off into the far corner of the garage, where a giant packing crate was filled with rolled-up socks. Emmy dug deep into the mound of socks until only her horn was visible.

"Where did my big book go?" Emmy said from beneath the socks.

Jesse glanced at the pile of children's story-books on the picnic table. "How about a *little* book?" he said brightly.

Emmy sniffed. "Okay, maybe. Read me, please," she said.

Daisy signaled to Jesse: they *had* to get to the computer and talk to Professor Andersson. Jesse replied with a firm shake of his head. Emmy still needed comforting, and this was part of the job.

"One story," Jesse told Emmy.

"One story," said Daisy.

"One story." Emmy's voice came back to them muffled by socks. "And maybe two. Not 'Hansel and Gretel.' Too scary."

While Daisy paced, Jesse selected one of Emmy's favorite books from the stack: *The Little Engine That Could.* By the time he got to the end, Emmy was sleeping soundly.

Jesse and Daisy tiptoed quickly out of the garage, making sure to lock both doors. Inside, they took off their shoes and ran up the stairs to the computer in Jesse's room. With Daisy standing behind him, Jesse sat at the keyboard and input the now-familiar Web address: www.foundadragon.org.

To their relief, the home page came up right away. The screen showed an illustration of a dragon and a picture of a very, very old man with a white beard, a mustache, and hair that was long, flowing, and white. Bushy white eyebrows threatened to overwhelm a fierce set of bright black eyes.

Jesse clicked the cursor on the old man's face, and the photograph came to life. "Ah, good day to you both! How may I be of service to my two stalwart young Dragon Keepers?" Professor Andersson asked, the corners of his eyes crinkling with a smile.

Jesse took a breath. "St. George left his lab at the college. And we have no idea where he went," he said in a rush.

The professor's eyebrows knit together. "Are you quite, quite certain?" he asked.

Jesse said, "Yeah. He's gone. Pulled up stakes. Flew the coop. Didn't leave a forwarding address. We don't know where he went or what he's up to."

The professor heaved a sigh and shook his head. "I doubt he has gone very far," he said.

Daisy stood over Jesse's right shoulder. She said, "What makes you so sure?"

"He might not know where the dragon is, but he knows where you are, and wherever you are, he knows the dragon can't be far away," said the professor. "Ergo, for better or for worse, St. George can never be very far away."

"Because St. George is thirsty for dragon blood," Jesse said with a little shudder.

"True enough," said the professor. "But you would do well not to focus quite so intently on the blood thirst. The imbibing of dragon blood is merely a means to an end."

"What end?" Daisy asked.

The professor explained. "The dragon is the only entity in creation that is in harmony with all four elements: air and water, fire and earth. Emmy's hatching, the first in more than a century, has brought about a remarkable occurrence. Her coming has reawakened the spirits of these elements."

"But isn't that a good thing?" Jesse asked.

"It would be, my boy, if St. George were not at large. The dragon herself is too young yet to keep St. George in check. As a result, no sooner do those magical spirits awaken than St. George will enslave them and draw upon their magic. When he has absorbed sufficient quantities of their magical essence, his power will be great. This is not a pleasant prospect."

Daisy paced behind Jesse's chair. "Fine, so what are *we* supposed to do about it?"

"Pay attention and follow the signs," said the professor. "I would suggest that the best place to start is with his first victims, the children of the earth."

Daisy stopped pacing. "The *who*?"

The computer screen flashed brightly and then went blank. Jesse didn't bother to try to get the site back. He knew that their visit with the professor had come to an end, unfortunately before they had gotten the answer to their last question.

Daisy let out a groan of frustration. Jesse rolled back in his chair and covered his face with his hands. Daisy continued to pace, her path extending now from Jesse's chair through the bathroom they shared, into her room, and back again. When she arrived at her bedroom window for the third time, she stopped and looked out. It had turned into such a beautiful day. It was hard to believe that bad stuff could be happening anywhere in the world when the sky stretched overhead like a vast blue circus tent.

"Children of the earth," she heard Jesse say in his deep-thinking voice. "What did he mean? Aren't we *all* children of the earth?"

At this, Daisy's glance dropped from the sky to the ground. *The earth.* Her eyes roamed the side yard, where the trees had visited earlier that day. And that was when she saw it, as clear as a highway on a road map.

"Jess, come look!" she called to him.

Jesse joined her. He looked out the window and saw it right away, too. "It's a trail," he said.

Daisy nodded excitedly. "Made of needles and leaves—"

"From a Douglas fir and a quaking aspen?" Jesse asked.

"Yep," said Daisy, "heading straight for the Dell, it looks like."

"Let's wake up Emmy and follow it," said Jesse.

Daisy grinned, and in thirty seconds flat the cousins were unlocking the garage door.

"Emmy is alllll better now!" Emmy told them when they'd gently shaken her awake. All traces of Emmy's jitters had vanished. She transformed back into her sheepdog shape, and they headed off to check out the trail of pine needles and leaves.

"Emmy," Jesse said, "you need to stay in your dog form when we get to the Dell. Something's up."

Emmy let out a cooperative little yip, and then raced along the trail that led up the backyard to the top of the rise. There they dropped to their knees and followed Emmy through the tunnel in the laurel bushes to the Dell. On the other side, they jumped to their feet, but the mysterious trail abruptly ended.

The Dell lay before them like a big bowl lined with wet clover and wildflowers, sparkling in the sunshine like a rainbow fallen to earth. On one side of the bowl was Old Mother Mountain. On the other side, not far from the overflowing stream, was the abandoned barn where Jesse and Daisy kept their Museum of Magic. Behind the barn lay the Deep Woods.

Emmy began barking, and Jesse and Daisy gasped. A wide ugly gouge, paved with wood chips and mud, cut into the heart of the Deep Woods. Felled trees lay everywhere like dead bodies.

"St. George is behind this," Jesse said through clenched teeth.

Emmy took off at a run, and the cousins ran after her, half sliding down the slope and across the squishy earth. Midway across the pasture, Daisy suddenly grabbed Jesse's arm and stopped him. "Look!" she said, pointing.

On either side of the ghastly gouge in the Deep Woods stood a tree—and around each tree trunk was a strip of cloth made from one of Miss Alodie's old flowered shirts.

"My *trees*, Jesse!" Daisy cried, jumping up and down and flapping her hands. "A Douglas fir and a quaking aspen! See?"

Emmy bounded around them, barking.

CHAPTER THREE

EARTHMOVERS

Daisy gripped Jesse and pulled him along as she walked right up to the Douglas fir. She shaded her eyes from the sun and called out, "Hellooooo!"

Jesse shook his head while Emmy sat, her tail a tiny happy blur. They waited.

The Douglas fir stood there silently, as trees usually do.

Daisy cupped her hands around her mouth. "Hey there!" she hollered. She stepped closer and rapped her knuckles on the trunk. "Hello, Douglas fir! We're here to help, if we can. Is anybody home? You know," she said to Jesse, "in my book on tree lore, it says the Douglas fir stands for wisdom and dignity."

Jesse squinted up at the tall fir. "I can see that," he said.

Emmy jumped up and circled the tree three times. Then she stopped, lifted her hind leg, and tinkled all over the base of the trunk.

"Emmy!" said Daisy. "That's not very polite!"

Jesse burst out laughing. "Sure it is. It's dragon piddle. It's probably magical," he said.

"Magical tinkle!" Daisy giggled.

Emmy trotted over to the quaking aspen and once again lifted her hind leg. She had saved a generous sprinkling of dragon piddle for the second tree.

"So what does the quaking aspen stand for?" Jesse asked.

Daisy stared up at the tree and thought a bit. "I want to say a bunch of waggling tongues, but I'm not sure. I'll have to look it up." Daisy walked over to the quaking aspen. "I apologize for my dog, er, dragon," she said.

For a second, it looked like the tree really *did* mind: its pale green leaves quivered indignantly in the breeze. But then the breeze died down and the leaves stopped moving.

Daisy sighed and stood back, hands on hips. "Maybe they just don't trust us yet."

"Maybe," said Jesse.

Emmy let out a sharp bark of disagreement.

"Then again," said Daisy, "maybe they just wanted us to see this mess."

"Well, now that we've seen it," said Jesse, "we have to do something about it!"

Emmy barked twice to say "Yes!" and started into the ravaged wood. Jesse and Daisy looked at each other. They didn't usually go into the Deep Woods. The woods were too dense and dark for casual walking. But there was nothing casual about this situation. They both nodded soberly and followed Emmy.

Five minutes later, the Deep Woods began to thin out, and the three came to what seemed to be a natural clearing. The clearing was about the size of three football fields. Jesse, Daisy, and Emmy crept to the edge of it and took cover behind the trunk of a tall spruce tree. Near their end of the clearing stood two supersize dump trucks, a steam shovel, and two bulldozers, all of them brand-new and painted bright orange. There didn't seem to be any workers around.

"What's that?" whispered Daisy, pointing to a huge machine off to the side that dwarfed all the others.

"It's an earthmover," Jesse whispered back. "I saw one once in Venezuela. It was mowing down the trees in the rain forest like they were matchsticks. I was really little, so at first I thought it was neat. Then my parents explained that the trees wouldn't grow back and that the forest and all the animals would be gone forever."

"So the Dragon Slayer is a Tree Slayer, too," Daisy said.

"I guess he can't do it with magic, so he needs these big machines. But where is he?" Jesse said, scanning the clearing. "He had to have done most of this work during the storm."

"I wonder why," Daisy said.

"Maybe so he wouldn't get caught," said Jesse. "Let's go check it out."

Daisy grabbed his sleeve. "No! Let's wait here until we're sure he's not lurking around," she said.

Jesse nodded. It could be a trap. He checked his watch. They would give it fifteen minutes, just to be safe. They waited in silence. Beneath Jesse's hand, Emmy trembled, but she sat between them patiently, her long pink forked tongue lolling out the side of her mouth.

As if Emmy had been keeping track of the time in her head, she jumped up and started into the clearing exactly fifteen minutes later. Jesse and Daisy were right behind her. Nose to the ground, Emmy made a beeline over to the foot of a huge mound of fresh, damp earth. Next to the mound was a hole. The cousins went over to it and peered down. The hole was wide and deep, and at the bottom, they caught a glimpse of open space, like an underground cave.

"What do you think it is?" Jesse asked, his voice eerily returning to him from the damp, dark hole.

"It looks like a mine," said Daisy grimly. "A very old, very deep mine."

"What does St. George want with a mine?" Jesse wondered aloud.

"I have no idea," Daisy said. "But let's get out of here before he comes back and shoves us in."

They walked back through the Deep Woods. At the edge, Daisy stopped and addressed the two trees. "We'll be back," she promised.

"With a real plan," Jesse added, and Emmy barked twice.

When they got back home, Emmy was hungry and tired. Safe inside the garage, she assumed her dragon form and looked at Jesse and Daisy expectantly. Jesse went into the house and returned a few minutes later with a head of kale, a bunch of spinach, and a chunk of Swiss cheese. Emmy made quick work of these and afterward, Jesse and Daisy tucked her into her nest of socks. Daisy read her "Goldilocks and the Three Bears" while Jesse leaned against the packing crate and listened.

Before Daisy reached the end of the story, Emmy's eyelids were drooping.

"Too much sudden activity after too many days of just lying around," Daisy said to Jesse out of the corner of her mouth, sounding just like her mother.

"That weather spell probably tuckered her out," Jesse replied with a yawn.

When Daisy closed the book, Emmy heaved a sleepy sigh and snuggled down into her bed of socks. "Emmy's bed is not too big and not too small. It is juuuuuuust right."

"For a while, at least," said Jesse. "Until Emmy-locks gets bigger."

"Sweet dragon dreams," said Daisy.

35

After the cousins had bid Emmy a final "good night, sleep tight" (even though it was still late afternoon), they tiptoed out of the garage and locked it. They both knew that if she needed them, she would bark very loudly three times and one of them would come running, even if it was the middle of the night.

Jesse and Daisy wearily trudged through the kitchen and upstairs. They were starved, but eating would have to wait. They went directly to Jesse's room and turned on the computer. Jesse sat down and logged on to the dragon site. They were both grateful to see that Professor Andersson was in the mood for another visit. With his bushy brows deeply furrowed, he listened as Jesse and Daisy briefed him about St. George's terrible path of destruction, the earthmover, and the hole leading down to the old mine.

"Old mines are dangerous places, and he's got all this heavy machinery and we're just a couple of kids, and . . . what are we supposed to do, professor?" Jesse said.

Daisy bumped Jesse with her hip and whispered, "You're whining. He hates whining."

But the professor didn't seem to notice. Usually, Jesse and Daisy saw only his face close-up, but now the professor moved away from the screen and leaned back in his chair. For the first time, they could see what he was wearing: an old-fashioned suit, a string tie, and suspenders. "I couldn't really say," said the professor, hooking his thumbs in his suspenders, which were red-and-white striped.

Jesse and Daisy stared at the screen. Here they were expecting an ominous warning or a stern lecture, or, at the very least, the barest of hints about what to do next.

"I'm a dragon man myself," the professor went on. "Ask me about masking, scrying, even spelling, and I'm the man for you. But mines and machines have always rather flummoxed me. They were never my forte."

Jesse turned to Daisy and asked, "What's a *fort* have to do with anything?"

Daisy shrugged, equally perplexed.

"Not my area of *expertise*," the professor explained. "Never cared much for mines, I must say. All those tunnels snaking beneath the earth make me feel claustrophobic. Closed in." The professor shivered.

"I feel the exact same way!" said Daisy, and just as she was about to tell him about her own worst encounter with enclosed spaces (getting stuck behind the claw-foot bathtub when she was three years old), the screen fizzled to a blank.

Jesse glowered at the computer and said, "Doesn't that man ever say 'good-bye' or 'over-and-out' or 'good night and good luck'?"

Just then, they heard Uncle Joe call them down to dinner.

Jesse and Daisy took a good look at themselves. They were covered with dried mud!

"Be there in five!" Daisy shouted, and they raced each other to the sink.

"I can't believe it turned into such a glorious day!" Aunt Maggie said, beaming at Jesse and Daisy across the dinner table.

"Raining one minute, sunny the next," Jesse said. "It was practically like magic!"

Daisy kicked him beneath the table. They had agreed upstairs not to tell the grown-ups about what was going on in the Dell. After all, the Dell was their special place. Its problems were their problems, not Daisy's parents'. "Poppy, tell us about the mines around here," Daisy said.

Uncle Joe gave his long graying ponytail an enthusiastic tug. If there was anything he liked more than talking about rocks, it was talking about mines. "The whole area is honeycombed with them. After all, this town was host to a prosperous gold mine operation in the early 1900s."

"We know that, Poppy," said Daisy. "That's how Goldmine City got its name."

"Yep, this whole area was overrun by prospectors burning up with gold fever. It was a boom city, with its own opera house and grand hotel and saloon and you name it, they had it. Then, practically overnight, the town shut down," he said with a thoughtful expression. "It was a ghost town until the 1970s, when the college came in and things began to look up again."

"Did the mine run out of gold?" Daisy asked. "Is that why Goldmine City turned into a ghost town?"

"Nope," said Uncle Joe. "The mine blew up."

"Blew up?" said Jesse, setting his milk glass down with a *clunk*.

"Kaboom," said Uncle Joe. "Some say the explosion was caused by underground gas. Others say it was a human being who caused it. Something to do with a feud."

"What kind of feud?" the cousins chimed in eagerly.

"A feud between the mining company and the farmer," said Uncle Joe, squeezing more ketchup and mustard onto his hamburger. "The farmer who worked the land behind this house, as a matter of fact."

"*Our* farmer?" Daisy asked.

"The Magical Dairyman?" Jesse whispered.

Uncle Joe snapped his fingers. "Now, what was his name? It'll come to me in a second. . . . Anyway, according to the stories, the farmer got all worked up and told everyone that the mining company was tunneling onto his land when they didn't have a claim," said Uncle Joe, biting into his burger.

"So what happened?" Daisy asked.

Uncle Joe shrugged and spoke with a full mouth. "The farmer blew the mine to smithereens, according to some people," he said, swallowing hard and smiling. "Buried the mine under so many tons of rubble, no one's ever dug back down. Oh, yeah, and the explosion killed the head of the mining company."

"Did the farmer get in trouble?" Jesse asked.

Uncle Joe shook his head. "The investigation was inconclusive. It might have been human mischief, but it might also have been natural gas. The farmer fled overseas. He's long dead now, of course—this was over a hundred years ago."

"Who owns the Dell now?" Jesse asked, stealing a look at Daisy.

Uncle Joe said, "That's a very good question. No one knows. The land's held in some kind of complicated trust. A bank in Switzerland pays the taxes every year, but no one knows who or where the current owners are . . . which is lucky for you guys, because you get the Dell all to yourselves."

"Not anymore, we don't," Jesse muttered as he dropped his half-eaten hamburger onto his plate.

Late that night, a sudden noise awoke Jesse. He sat up in bed and blinked at the clock until it came into focus. It was two o'clock in the morning, but the full moon lit up his room like daylight. He went over to the window and looked out.

Emmy was standing in the driveway, staring right back up at him. She was in full dragon form, her beautiful blue-green scales resplendent in the moonlight. Jesse's heart pounded. They had been careful, as always, to lock her in the garage. How had she gotten out?

Jesse jammed his feet into his sneakers, ran through the bathroom to Daisy's room, and shook her awake.

"Emmy's out," he told her in a loud whisper. "Get your sneakers on!"

"Yikes!" Daisy popped up and peeled away the covers, her hair a nest of snarls. She groped around under the bed for her sneakers and fumbled with the laces. Then the two of them tiptoed down the stairs and through the kitchen. They opened and closed the back door, careful not to let it slam.

Then they ran down the path toward the dragon in the driveway. Daisy whispered frantically, "Emmy! What are you doing? What if someone sees you?"

"No one sees me," Emmy hissed back at Daisy. "Mrs. Nosy-Britches is fast asleep in her nest."

"How did you get out?" Jesse wanted to know.

"My new friends opened the door," Emmy said happily. "I love them."

"New friends?" Jesse asked.

"What new friends?" Daisy asked.

"Those new friends," said Emmy, waving her arms toward the trellis by the side of the garage.

Two figures as tall as trees towered in the dappled shadows. Daisy gasped and reached out for Jesse's arm as one of the figures stepped forward into the moonlight. His hair was long and dark and snarled and full of pine needles. His feet were bare. His toes were very dirty, tinged with green, twice as long as anyone's toes ever grow to be, and covered with long pale hairs.

"I'm Douglas Fir," he said in a voice that was powerful yet full of warmth. A waft of clean, fresh pine air enveloped the cousins, and they found themselves taking great deep breaths of it.

"And this is my lovely companion," said Douglas Fir. "Lady Aspen."

A second towering figure strode to his side. She

was as tall as he was, but where he was greenish brown, she was as pale as paper. Her head was wreathed with little round leaves that shook when she walked. Her voice shook, too, as she said, "H-h-h-hello, D-d-d-d-dragon K-k-k-k-keepers. It is a pleasure to m-m-make your acq-q-q-q-quaintance."

Jesse stared hard at the two figures and realized he could actually see right through them to the trellis. Their images shifted and wavered with the evening breeze, breaking apart like reflections on the surface of a pond. They were wrapped in coarse fabric—his green, hers white—and around both their middles were sashes made from brightly colored fabric.

"Wow!" said Jesse. "Tree spirits."

"Dryads!" said Daisy.

"Yes, Jesse Tiger and Daisy Flower," said Emmy proudly. "You have hit the nail on the bull's-eye."

"On the head," Jesse corrected automatically.

"On the bull's head," Emmy said. "In The Time Before, the dryads and the dragons were like family, like Jesse and Daisy, like cousins."

Daisy asked the trees, "Why didn't you talk to us when we saw you in the woods?"

"We speak more clearly when our spirits break away from our bodies," Lady Aspen explained. "Our bodies, y-y-you see, are back at the edge of the Deep Woods. Our spirits can wander. We c-c-c-can't always leave our bodies during the d-d-d-daylight hours."

"The moonlight helps to draw us out," Douglas explained. "And that squirt of dragon piddle must have helped, too."

"Did Miss Alodie give you those sashes?" Jesse wanted to know.

"S-s-s-she did indeed," said the aspen.

"We're very lucky that she did. The charm she put on them warded off St. George's spell," the fir explained.

Daisy turned to Jesse. "I knew it! Didn't I always say that Miss Alodie was magic?"

Jesse shrugged and grinned. "I just thought she was wacky."

Lady Aspen broke in, "W-w-w-we are the only t-t-t-trees in the Deep Woods that have n-n-n-not fallen under the power of St. G-g-g-g-eorge. Follow us, p-please. There is n-n-no m-m-more time to lose."

"In our pajamas?" Daisy asked.

"The moon won't mind," said Douglas Fir. "And we won't, either."

"It's a pajama parade!" Emmy said.

"Pajama *party*," Jesse corrected.

Emmy looked sad. "But where are *my* pajamas?" she asked.

"You don't need pajamas, Emmy," Daisy told her. "You have beautiful green and blue scales!"

"That's true, I am very beautiful," Emmy said, recovering her good spirits. "Let's go!"

The tree spirits wheeled around and headed into the backyard, with Emmy trotting along between them. The cousins followed them across the grass, which was so wet with dew that their pajamas were soon soaked up to the knees. When they came to the laurel bushes, the dryads stepped over them like circus performers on stilts, while the cousins and Emmy burrowed through the tunnel. Daisy thought she heard a faint whispering in the laurel leaves as they brushed past them. "Jessssssssssssseeeeeee! Daissssssseeeeeeeeee! Helllp ussssssss."

The cousins had been to the Dell at night a few times. How hushed and magical it had been then, with the peepers' voices throbbing in the dark greenery. Now a harsh blue-white light shone out from the heart of the Deep Woods. Instead of the throbbing of peepers, the air was filled with the ominous rumble and roar of heavy machinery.

Douglas Fir and Lady Aspen stood waiting

while Jesse and Daisy and Emmy took it all in.

"So that's why St. George wasn't around the college this afternoon," Jesse said. "He works at night."

"Why would he do that?" Daisy asked.

"Because he's a bad, bad man," Emmy said in a fierce whisper.

"And because what he's doing is illegal. You heard your dad. This isn't his land," Jesse said.

"It's the farmer's land," Daisy said, nodding. "And the farmer's not here, so we're going to have to represent his interests."

Jesse gave her a weird look. "Really?"

Daisy grinned. "I don't know. But it sounded good, didn't it?" she said. "Let's go."

The motley group, led by the trees, marched down the hill and across the pasture, over to the path that led into the Deep Woods.

"You must take matters in hand now," said Douglas Fir. "Start by climbing us," he said as his transparent spirit stepped back into the solid trunk of the tree.

"P-p-please do," said Lady Aspen as she, too, disappeared into her pale trunk.

Jesse turned to Emmy. "Did they just say to climb them?"

Emmy shook her head and nodded in rapid

succession. "Yes. No. Dragons do not climb trees. Yes, boys and girls do. Boys climb boys and girls climb girls," she said, as if it were common knowledge.

Jesse looked up. The lowest branches of the Douglas fir were way over his head and the trunk was too wide to shimmy up. Just as Jesse was about to protest that it wasn't possible, he found himself engulfed by pine needles as the tree bent over him and picked him up into its branches. The quaking aspen did the same for Daisy.

Jesse wrapped his arms around a stout branch.

"Look at me!" Daisy called softly from her perch in the crown of the quaking aspen.

Jesse could make out her silvery hair shimmering among the pale green leaves, and then her hand waved in the moonlight. "Whoa!" he said, hanging on tightly as the Douglas fir uprooted itself with a soft grunt and began to move over the debris-ridden path. When he was eight years old in India, Jesse had ridden in an elephant's howdah, one of those fancy cushioned saddles with the tasseled canopies. He discovered that if he let go and went with the motion of the elephant, it could be quite comfortable. Applying the same principle to the tree, he relaxed and began to sway along.

Jesse caught the occasional glimpse of Emmy's

moonstruck scales as she kept pace with them, moving steadily under cover of the trees of the Deep Woods.

The light ahead grew brighter and the noise of the machinery grew louder, and the trees slowed down. Finally, they came to a silent standstill at the edge of the clearing.

St. George was there.

CHAPTER FOUR

ENTER THE SHOVEL

He stood in the bed of a giant dump truck like an actor on a movie set, every detail of his handsome face visible beneath a circle of powerful spotlights blazing from atop high metal stalks. He wore his usual long black coat. A bright orange hard hat sat incongruously on his head, his golden hair spilling to his shoulders beneath it. His round wire-rimmed spectacles reflected the glare of the lights and made him look as if he had a slice of cucumber over each eye. He was pointing with a gloved hand and shouting to a crew of workers in orange jumpsuits.

A steam shovel rumbled and swiveled on its base as it reached down into the hole. The scoop came up and swiveled back, dumping its load on top of the dirt mound, which had risen to mountainous proportions since the afternoon. A worker scrambled up out of the hole. He was covered in muck, a pickax slung over his shoulder. The muddy cuffs of his orange jumpsuit drooped around his ankles.

At first Jesse thought he was looking at a child dressed up in a grown man's work clothes. Cautiously, he shimmied out to the end of the branch to get a closer look.

He sucked in his breath. It *wasn't* a child. The muddy figure in the orange jumpsuit was broad and stocky through the shoulders. The worker used his pick to swing himself up onto the back of the dump truck. In a rolling gait, he made his way over to St. George. He was an odd-looking little man, with a huge head that was flat and wide on top, like an anvil. His bristly hair grew down to a point between his tiny eyes, which were deeply set on either side of his large smashed snout. When the man flung an arm out to gesture at the hole, Jesse thought at first that he wore mittens. Then he realized that the man had only three fingers on his hand!

Jesse looked over to Daisy, who had also moved out to the end of a branch to get a better look. Jesse tried to catch her eye, but she looked totally absorbed in the scene before them. Jesse checked out the other workers. There were at least forty of them swarming over the site and, except for slight differences in height and weight and hair color, they all looked alike.

St. George leaped down from the bed of the truck and climbed up into the cab. He gunned the engine and the truck jerked forward. The little man in back grabbed on to the side of the truck as it rumbled across the clearing. On the far side, Jesse could just barely make out a sort of lumber mill where workers were feeding logs into a saw.

Jesse felt the needles on the branches all around begin to prick him, as if the spirit inside the tree were asking, "Well? Do you think you have seen enough?"

"Let's get out of here," he whispered.

The fir and the aspen began to back up very slowly, then they melted away down the path.

Emmy was already waiting for them at the edge of the Deep Woods when the trees lowered Jesse and Daisy down to the ground. Jesse's hands and hair were sticky with pine sap. Daisy shook a small cascade of aspen leaves out of her snarled hair. They went to Emmy.

Emmy jumped up and down with excitement. "Did you see? Did you see?"

"Did you see their heads?" said Daisy with a shiver. "It's like they were made to be stacked upside down. And those icky, tiny little eyes!"

"They had snouts!" Jesse said.

"I have a snout," Emmy said, her enthusiasm rapidly dimming.

"What about their hands?" Daisy said, and held up her fingers to make mittens.

Jesse did the same and they pretended to shake hands with their mittens, giggling. Emmy did not join in.

The transparent dryads emerged from the solid trunks of their trees and floated over to join them.

Lady Aspen said gently, "B-b-b-beware, lest you judge any living creature b-b-based on physical appearance alone."

"What the lady says is true," Douglas Fir joined in. "St. George is a fine figure of a man, and yet we know for a fact that inside he is as rotten as a tree stump in a beaver colony's rank backwater."

"Listen to my new friends," said Emmy crossly. "It's not nice to make fun. I think the little men are pretty."

Daisy wheeled on Emmy. "How can you say that? They're working with St. George!"

"That makes them as bad as he is," Jesse said.

Emmy burst into tears.

Daisy and Jesse exchanged startled looks. They went to hug her. "We're sorry, Em," said Daisy.

"You're a little tired, I guess," said Jesse.

"And we're all up way past our bedtime," Daisy added.

Emmy nodded rapidly. "I need my cozy nest of socks," she said.

"I think we've all seen enough for one night," said Douglas Fir, heaving a heavy, pine-laden sigh. "We will walk you back to your house."

As they made their way across the pasture toward home, Jesse and Daisy continued to talk about the creatures. "Revolting little pig-men!" Daisy exclaimed.

"Th-th-th-they are n-n-n-not *pig-men*," Lady Aspen gently said. "They are the chthonic ones."

"What's 'chthonic'?" Jesse asked.

"A race of beings that live in a kingdom f-f-far

b-b-b-beneath us," the aspen said shakily, "in the b-b-b-bowels of the earth."

Jesse shook his head sadly. "Unless we come up with a truly *serious* plan, we're doomed! It was bad enough when we had St. George to deal with," he said. "Now we've got . . . those flat-headed, hairy little pig-people."

"Don't call them that!" Emmy scolded. "Call them hobgoblins!"

Daisy pulled up short. "Really?" she said.

The dryads nodded solemnly.

"You see?" said Jesse. "That proves it. Everyone knows hobgoblins are bad."

"Everyone thinks dragons are bad, too," Emmy said in a small voice.

"Oh, that's just because they haven't met you," said Daisy.

After tucking Emmy into her nest of socks, the cousins stumbled into the house and upstairs. They each fell into their beds and sank into a sleep so deep, they didn't wake up until they smelled break-fast cooking downstairs.

Daisy got dressed quickly and went into Jesse's room. Jesse, already dressed, was scowling at the computer screen, which refused to produce Profes-sor Andersson's site, even after repeated attempts.

Finally, he turned from the empty screen and said one word: "Hobgoblins."

Daisy smiled and looked relieved. "I thought maybe I'd dreamed it."

"If only," said Jesse.

They went downstairs and joined Uncle Joe and Aunt Maggie at the kitchen table. As she nibbled at a crispy strip of bacon, Daisy asked her father the same question she would have asked the professor, had he been available. "Poppy, what's 'chthonic' mean?"

"Whoa, Nelly!" said Uncle Joe, dropping his fork with a clatter. "You're poaching on my territory now. 'Chthonic' comes from the ancient Greek *chthon,* which means 'earth' or 'soil.' You could say that rocks and minerals and crystals are of the chthonic world, because they come from the earth. But the word is usually linked with chthonic deities, which in the olden times were the gods of the underworld, otherwise known," he said, with a wicked little grin, "as the dead."

Jesse wagged his head woefully and said under his breath, "I knew it! Those guys are bad news."

"'Chthonic'!" Uncle Joe chuckled. "Where in Sam Hill did you guys dig up that word?"

Daisy shrugged. "Online," she said.

"You've got to watch that online stuff," said

Uncle Joe. "Not everything you read is true, and there are an awful lot of cranks out there."

At the mention of "cranks," Aunt Maggie's head shot up from her plate and her eyes narrowed. "You two aren't talking to strangers online, are you?"

Daisy's eyes went wide. Jesse kicked her beneath the table.

"Never!" Daisy said, her elfin ears going all pink.

Jesse sat up tall and said, "Not us!" After all, Professor Andersson might be strange, but he was not a stranger.

Aunt Maggie went off to work muttering about creepy online strangers, and Uncle Joe headed for the Rock Shop. Jesse washed the breakfast dishes and Daisy rummaged in the refrigerator for breakfast for Emmy while they conferred about their next steps. If the professor wasn't available, maybe Miss Alodie could explain more about the sashes around the trees. Then Jesse delivered Emmy her breakfast and left Daisy to pack their backpack with the day's supplies: five energy bars, a canteen of water, and a head of cabbage for Emmy. As soon as Emmy finished her breakfast, they lit out, with her in dog form, for Miss Alodie's house.

They saw Miss Alodie's green beanie, which looked like the top of a zucchini, bobbing along the line of rosebushes. The roses seemed like their spiffy old selves, and the black-eyed Susans had their heads on straight again. The garden, however, still had the weird fence surrounding it.

On the way over, Daisy had already decided on the direct approach, so she stepped over the fence and marched around the roses, right up to Miss Alodie. Pointing a finger at the little woman, Daisy said, "We know that you're magic."

Miss Alodie's blue eyes danced as she tucked her garden shears into one of the many pockets of her fisherman's vest. "Well, now, what gave me away? Was it my glittering wand or my blue wizard's hat with the silver stars on it?"

Jesse didn't so much as crack a smile. "It was this fence, right here," he said sternly.

"Plus the cloth you wrapped around those two trees," Daisy said. "You know the ones I'm talking about: the Douglas fir and the quaking aspen. Both the fence and the tree sashes are charms to ward off St. George's spell, so there's no use denying it. And let's not forget, there's this superhumanly gorgeous garden of yours."

"How do you know I'm not just a cracking good gardener?" Miss Alodie asked with a lingering twinkle in her blue eyes.

"Because you talk to your flowers," said Daisy.

"And they probably talk back to you," added Jesse.

Miss Alodie threw back her head and laughed until her blue eyes were bright with tears. "Well put, cousins!" she said at last. "Would you care to come inside for a tisane and some fairy cake so we can further discuss matters magical?"

No way was Jesse ready for that. "Uh. We're good," he said, backing away.

"We just had breakfast," Daisy said. "And we don't really have time."

And then it all came tumbling out, as first Daisy and then Jesse told Miss Alodie *everything*. "I guess you can see why we need your help," Daisy said in conclusion.

Miss Alodie cocked an eyebrow and regarded them for several moments. "Poor defenseless little children," she said after a pause. "But listen to me, you two. You are a far cry from helpless. Not with an entire Museum of Magic at your disposal!"

Jesse and Daisy turned to look at each other. Then they looked back at her.

"Go on with you," she told them, shooing them back to the curb. "Check your inventory. And remember, no matter how bad things get, you have *dragon magic* on your side."

Emmy barked in agreement. Jesse and Daisy were leaving when Miss Alodie called out, "Wait! I do have a thing or two to give you . . . *if* you do one thing for *me*."

They turned around. In one hand Miss Alodie held out a big ball of string. In the other was a jar full of fat pink wriggling earthworms. Daisy took the string and left the jar for Jesse.

"Thanks, Miss Alodie," Jesse said dutifully. "What do you want us to do?"

Miss Alodie's face went flat. "I want that book," she said in a low, urgent voice.

"What book?" said Daisy blankly.

"The big book?" Jesse asked slowly.

Jesse raised an eyebrow at Daisy. St. George's big book was just possibly the one detail they had left out of their story.

"You mean the great big book covered in red leather?" Daisy asked. "The one with the iron ring on the cover and the funny gold writing all over it?"

Miss Alodie nodded solemnly. "The very one. I want you to bring it back to me."

Emmy barked enthusiastically. The cousins looked at her carefully. Of course. Emmy wanted the book, too. Hadn't she said so just the day before?

Daisy laughed uneasily. "Okay, but how are we going to get it? It's way too heavy for us to carry," she said.

"When the moment is right, unscrew the lid of the jar and let the worms out," Miss Alodie said.

Daisy shook her head slowly. "Why? And what would be the right moment, exactly?" she asked.

Jesse turned so that Daisy could unzip the backpack and tuck away Miss Alodie's gifts.

Miss Alodie was already back at work, down on her hands and knees, pulling up weeds. "Oh, you'll know the right moment when it comes."

"*How* will we know?" Jesse asked, resettling the weight on his back.

Miss Alodie looked up, her blue eyes dancing. "Oh, you'll know . . . I'm sure of it . . . two brave, resourceful Dragon Keepers like yourselves. Something will surely hit you. And incidentally, they are devas."

"What are day-vahs?" the cousins both asked at once.

"The spirits of the flowers you say I talk to," said Miss Alodie with a wink. "Call them devas."

Checking their magical inventory was the first order of business. So Jesse, Daisy, and Emmy went directly to the barn from Miss Alodie's house. Even though they were pretty sure that St. George wouldn't be around during daylight hours, just to be on the safe side, they asked Emmy to wait until they were inside the barn before she transformed. Daisy slid the heavy barn door shut behind them, Jesse set down the backpack, and Emmy turned into a dragon.

"Please come here, Emmy," said Daisy, going over to the Museum of Magic. "You're the one with the dragon magic, so you try first. Is there anything here that looks useful . . . practical in a magical kind of way?"

Emmy shuffled up to the display, which was arranged across some old boards on top of two saw-horses.

"I like *this* one," said Emmy, reaching out and taking up her favorite item, the crusty old metal ball about the size of a peach, and cradling it in her paws.

"The Sorcerer's Sphere," Jesse said in an encouraging tone.

"I like it a lot!" said Emmy brightly.

"We know you like it," Daisy said patiently. "You always have. But what we want to know is . . . are we supposed to *use* it—against St. George and his minions?"

Emmy shut her eyes and then opened them

61

quickly. She shook her head. "Not now. I am sorry, Daisy and Jesse. I am not a very practical dragon."

Jesse pressed her gently. "You're one hundred percent *certain* sure?"

Emmy nodded. "Cross my heart and hope to die, stick a beetle in my eye," she said.

"It's *needle*," Jesse corrected. "Stick a needle in your eye."

"Ouch," said Emmy, flinching. "That would give me a very bad boo-boo, wouldn't it?"

"Yes, it would," said Daisy. "So maybe you'd better not be swearing it. Okay, now I guess it's my turn to try."

While Jesse and Emmy looked on anxiously, Daisy closed her eyes and held her hands out over their magical collection. She waved them slowly over the rocks and feathers and skulls and horseshoes and doorknobs, hoping to feel a tug in one direction or another, like on a Ouija board. After what seemed like a very long time, she opened her eyes and shook her head. "Guess I'm not very practical, either. You try, Jess." She stood aside.

Instead of closing his eyes and doing the Ouija board routine, Jesse simply drifted around the table, looking at the items as he went, giving each one the full power of his concentration. He had homed in on the green crystal doorknob when something bumped him so hard, it knocked the breath clean out of him.

"Ouch!" he said, rubbing his shoulder and looking around with a frown. "Who did that?"

Daisy and Emmy both stared at him in amazement.

"Did you see that?!" Daisy asked.

"The shovel fell down on you, *crash-bang-boom!*" said Emmy, clapping her paws in amusement.

"It just . . . fell off the wall where it was hanging and hit you!" Daisy said. "Nobody even touched it! Look!"

Jesse looked down at the rusty old shovel lying at his feet. He looked up at the wall where a bunch of rusty old farm implements hung. They had never paid much attention to these tools. Sometimes they thought the tools might be magic, but most of the time they just figured they were old and maybe even a little dangerous.

Reaching down, Jesse picked up the shovel by its worn wooden handle. He cried out as the shovel jerked him forward with a violence that nearly dislocated his arm. It was as if someone, a mighty strong someone, were yanking the shovel for all he—or she or it—was worth.

"It's pulling me!" he shouted to the others, feeling scared and happy at the same time. "What should I do?"

"Yikes!" said Daisy, dancing nervously in place. "Hang on tight, I guess. See where it takes you."

Jesse held on to the handle with both hands as the shovel powered him out through the barn's sliding door.

"Stay with me!" he hollered over his shoulder. "Please don't let it run away with me!"

"You are a very brave boy, Jesse Tiger!" said Emmy. "Emmy Dragon loves you."

"Daisy Flower does, too!" Daisy said breathlessly. "And we're right behind you, don't worry!"

They followed him outside to where a ramp ran up the side of the barn to a door that was boarded shut. There, not ten feet from the barn, the earth rose in a gentle grassy hummock. The shovel blade rocketed skyward. For a brief giddy moment, Jesse's feet dangled in midair. *The shovel is shooting me right to the sun!* he thought. Then the blade came swooping back around and sank itself into the heart of the grassy hummock. After that, it proceeded to do what shovels do best: it started digging.

"It's digging a hole!" Daisy exclaimed in wonder, watching as the shovel dug into the earth, scooped up dirt, and heaved it off to one side, dragging Jesse along with it like a rag doll.

"Guess I better hang on!" Jesse shouted to Daisy and Emmy. "It's way stronger than I am!"

"Do the best you can!" Daisy called to him.

Then Emmy said, "I will be a dog and dig with my puppy paws," transforming into her dog shape and beginning to dig enthusiastically alongside the team of Jesse and Shovel.

The hole got deeper and the mound of dirt higher as both Jesse's shovel and Emmy's front paws burrowed their way into the earth. Jesse wanted to reach up and wipe off the sweat that was stinging his eyes, but he was afraid to let go. True to her word, Daisy stuck by him. She stood on the sidelines and watched, arms raised to protect herself from the storm of flying earth while she called out encouragement.

For at least an hour, the digging went on. It wasn't long before Jesse was so tired and dizzy that he shut his eyes. And just as he was drifting off into a feverish swoon, the shovel flew up out of the hole and planted itself in the loose dirt.

Jesse opened his eyes. He staggered out of the hole and sagged against the shovel.

Daisy ran and brought him back a cup of icy cold water from the old pump.

Jesse pried one stiff hand off the shovel, took the cup, and drained it in one gulp. "Another," he gasped, holding out the cup.

Daisy got another.

He poured this one over his head, still leaning on the handle of the shovel. He hadn't quite caught his breath yet and his legs were weak and wobbly.

"I know . . . that the shovel . . . did most of the work . . . but I still don't think I've ever worked this hard . . . in my whole life," he said to Daisy between deep, shaky breaths.

"You were great," Daisy said. "Emmy, too. Oh, look!"

Emmy lay on the barn ramp, too tired to turn back into a dragon, with her pink forked tongue lolling out of her mouth and her filthy furry side heaving.

"Poor thing! I'd better get some water for her, too," Daisy said, taking the cup and returning to the pump.

"Get one for my shovel while you're at it!" Jesse called out to Daisy, and she let out a nervous hoot of laughter.

Gingerly, Jesse left the shovel in the dirt and looked at the palms of his hands. They were dotted with white blisters. He blew on them. "Well, I think that's enough digging for one day," he said.

As if in response, the shovel pulled itself out of the dirt, moved back down into the hole, and continued digging all by itself. The next minute, the shovel began to make scraping noises.

"I wish I'd known it could dig by itself," Jesse said as he peered down into the hole. "Is that wood?" he asked.

Daisy and Emmy, dragon-formed once again, went to the edge of the hole and stared down into it. The shovel had, indeed, uncovered something that looked very much like wood. The shovel stopped and stood aside, as if to give them all a chance to get a good look.

"It's old wood," Daisy said.

"Painted wood," said Jesse.

The shovel went back to work now, only more slowly and carefully than before. It became obvious to the cousins and their dragon that the shovel was digging up a door: a plain wooden door, painted pale green. Soon the door was completely uncovered and surrounded on all four sides by a neat trench. It lay in the earth, an inviting rectangle set on a slight angle, with the high end sloping upward, toward the barn.

CHAPTER FIVE

THE DOOR IN THE EARTH

The shovel rose up in the air, spun around several times, and buried its blade once again in the mound of loose dirt as if to say, "Ta-da!"

Jesse waited a moment, then went over and, blisters and all, pulled the shovel out of the dirt. He hefted it. "The magic's gone," he said to the other two in wonder. "It feels like a regular old shovel now."

"That's because it's allllll done!" said Emmy happily.

"If it's finished digging, maybe we should hang it back on the wall, where it belongs," Daisy suggested.

"Okay," said Jesse, taking the shovel back into the barn. When he rejoined them by the side of the hole, they continued to stand there and stare down.

"I guess we should get in there and check it out," said Jesse finally.

"I guess," said Daisy dubiously.

Jesse slid on his behind down into the hole. Standing in the trench to one side of the door, Jesse bent down and examined it. Where the doorknob should have been, there was only a hole. He put his eye to the hole and peered in. He had a sensation of open space. It was definitely a door that led somewhere. He put his nose to the hole and sniffed. It smelled musty, like roots and rot and something slightly fruity.

Jesse hooked two fingers into the knob hole and tugged hard. The door wouldn't open. He ran his fingers along the side of the door and tried to lift it like the lid of a large chest. But the door held fast.

Above him, on her hands and knees, Daisy stared down at him, with Emmy peering brightly over her shoulder. A grin slowly spread across Daisy's face. "You know what you need?" she asked. "A *doorknob*! And I've got just the one for you." She leaped to her feet with such enthusiasm that she sent a small shower of dirt pattering down onto Jesse's face.

Daisy returned holding the green crystal doorknob from their Museum of Magic collection.

"One Magic Doorknob, coming up. Catch," said Daisy, tossing it down to Jesse.

He caught it. Then he bent down and fit it into the hole in the door. It slipped in smoothly, fit perfectly, and turned with a smart, satisfying *click*. Jesse pulled the knob. The door opened a crack. Heart hammering, Jesse opened it the rest of the way with a loud, long, rusty creak. A gust of earthen-smelling air enveloped him. Through the open door he saw a set of stone stairs leading steeply downward into darkness.

"We've got some stairs here," Jesse announced to the others. "Let's see where they lead, okay?"

"Oh, goody!" Emmy called down to him.

When he didn't hear anything from Daisy, he

turned and looked. She was rising slowly to her feet, backing away from the edge of the hole. Jesse scrambled out after her.

"Wait'll you see how neat these stairs are, Daze!" Jesse said.

Daisy had a very odd look on her face.

"That knob . . . it fit the door like it was made for it. It's magic!" Jesse paused, then asked, "What's the matter, Daisy?"

"What if it's the *wrong* kind of magic?" she asked in a small voice.

Jesse looked down through the doorway and then up at Daisy. "First the shovel, then the door, then the knob, now the stairs . . . Daisy, we can't stop now. Don't you see? *Going down the stairs is the right thing to do.*"

Daisy shivered and held her elbows tightly. "I never told you this, but when I was little, I got wedged behind Grandma's claw-foot bathtub. I crawled back there to find my ball. I was stuck there for hours until they found me. They had to pour olive oil all over me to pull me out. Ever since then, I've had a thing about tight, dark spaces. . . ." She looked into the doorway. "Like *that*. I don't think I can go down there."

"I can!" said Emmy merrily. "I think I can, I

think I can, I think I can," she said as she slid into the hole, turned herself neatly around, and began to back down the stairs.

"Be very, very careful!" Daisy called to Emmy.

Emmy stopped chanting. "Don't worry. I am a very careful dragon," she called back. Then she resumed the chant as she lowered herself down the stairs.

The cousins watched her disappear, her golden voice echoing out of the darkness. "I think I can. I think I can. . . ."

Then the chanting faded away.

Daisy gasped and fell to her knees, shouting through the doorway. "Emmy! Say something! Emmy? Jess, she's not saying anything. I'm going down there." Daisy swiveled onto her backside and was just about to slide down into the hole when Emmy's eager face appeared in the doorway. Her great green eyes shone with wonder and excitement.

"Jesse, Daisy, come down now!" she said with such urgency that Jesse dropped down beside Daisy and they both scooted into the hole and through the door. Jesse went down the stairs first, but Daisy wasn't far behind.

It was at least ten degrees cooler down there. The cousins found their arms immediately covered with gooseflesh. Hugging themselves, they stood at the bottom of the stairs and looked around. They appeared to be in a small room.

"This isn't so scary," said Daisy. There was just enough space for all three of them to stand in a small square room where old wooden shelves lined three of the walls. The shelves were crowded with ancient mason jars full of tomatoes and peaches and green beans and other things impossible to recognize in the dim light.

"It's the farmer's old root cellar," said Daisy as she turned in a slow circle.

"Yep," Jesse agreed, feeling a tug of disappointment.

"I don't know about you guys, but this doesn't seem very magical to me," Daisy said. "It's just old and musty and cold. Let's go back up, where it's warm and sunny."

"I guess," Jesse said with a sigh.

"NO!" cried Emmy, with such ferocity that the cousins gaped at her. Her pale green belly heaved. Her tail whipped back and forth.

"Whoa," said Jesse. He knew the signs: Emmy was about to fly into one of her tantrums.

"I want to stay!" Emmy said fiercely, her body quaking.

"Emerald," Jesse said in a low, stern voice. He

made calming motions with his hands. "Look. You can't stay down here. We've already seen all there is to see, and besides, it's probably not safe. And don't even *think* about eating the stuff in these jars."

Emmy backed up. "I have to stay."

The shelves behind her rattled as she bumped against them. The next lash of her tail swept all the mason jars off the bottom two shelves. They thudded to the dirt floor and rolled every which way underfoot.

"Watch out for exploding jars!" Daisy said, grabbing her head. "The stuff inside might have gone bad."

But Jesse couldn't worry about that now. "Emmy, please come back up with us."

"I WILL STAY!" she thundered, taking another step backward. Her hind legs began to slip and slide on the jars. She tumbled into the shelves behind her. With a wrenching, wood-splintering crash, they gave way. A shower of dirt sifted down from above.

"The sky is falling!" shouted Emmy.

Daisy screamed and covered her head. "We're all going to be buried alive!"

When the dirt shower tapered off, the cousins and Emmy looked around. The wall of shelves behind Emmy was gone. Beyond the shelves was an open space, extending into a tunnel. The tunnel, framed by ancient timbers, was no wider than a doorway and just high enough to fit Emmy, with very little room to spare.

"This isn't just a root cellar," Daisy said. "It's the entrance to the old mine."

"I know!" said Jesse.

"Let's go in the old mine, Clementine!" Emmy sang.

"Oh, my darlin', I'm right behind you!" said Jesse.

"Are you guys *nuts*?!" Daisy exploded.

Jesse and Emmy stared at Daisy, both looking a little hurt.

"You guys don't understand," Daisy said. "You didn't grow up here. Every kid in this town has been told, since we were practically born, to stay away from the old mines. They're very dangerous places. If Poppy knew we had dug up an old mine . . . he'd be so mad at us. . . ." She shivered.

Jesse was silent for a few seconds. Then he said, "Do you think he'd still feel that way if he knew we were going into the mine . . . with a dragon?"

Just over Jesse's shoulder, Emmy nodded her head vigorously in support of his argument.

Daisy sighed.

"And that the hole into the mine was dug with a magic shovel?" Jesse said with a sly grin.

"Listen to Jesse Tiger, Daisy Flower," said Emmy.

Daisy folded her arms across her chest and scowled at them.

"And that we are battling against a man who wants to suck all the magic out of the world and make it his?" Jesse added.

"All right!" Daisy held up both hands in surrender. "You two wait right here while I go back to the barn and get the backpack. I'm pretty sure there's a flashlight in it. If I'm going to do this crazy thing, I want to at least be able to see where I'm going."

Jesse and Emmy fairly hummed with excitement while they stood at the entrance to the mine and waited for Daisy to come back. She returned a few minutes later with the backpack. While she was gone, she had tied a purple bandanna around her head. Jesse stared at it questioningly.

"Bats," she explained. "Aren't old mines always filled with bats?"

Jesse shrugged. "I wouldn't know. This is my first time."

Daisy set the backpack down, zipped it open,

and poked around inside. "One of the energy bars is squished," she said.

"I'll eat that one," Jesse volunteered cheerfully.

"And this cabbage head is starting to stink," said Daisy, wrinkling her nose.

"Stinky cabbage is my favorite!" Emmy said.

Daisy continued to rummage. "We also have the jar of magic earthworms Miss Alodie gave us, plus one big ball of string. How useful."

"Are you kidding?" Jesse said. "The string will be perfect!"

"For what?" Daisy asked.

"To leave a trail of string behind us. If the tunnel branches out into more tunnels, we'll be able to find our way back out."

"You hope," said Daisy.

Jesse forged ahead optimistically. "Look, Daze, what's the worst thing that can happen to us?"

"We run into St. George and his band of vicious hobgoblins?" Daisy said grouchily.

"St. George's onions," Emmy said with a sage nod of her head.

"Minions," Daisy corrected with a reluctant smile. Finally, she found the flashlight. She shook it, rattling the battery in the cylinder, and then switched it on. "When was the last time we changed the batteries?" she asked Jesse.

"Last week," Jesse replied. "So that means we're all set to go."

"Almost," said Daisy. She pulled the dog leash out of the backpack. "Emmy, you're going to have to wear this while we're in the mine."

"Not that old stinker," said Emmy, rearing back. "Not me. Leashes are for *dogs*. Emmy is a *dragon princess!*"

Daisy said, "Sure. Fine. Have it your way, Your Majesty. No leash, no mine. It's your choice. 'Cause we can't have you gallivanting around loose down here in the dark."

"But Daisy Flower has a very bright flashlight, so it will not be dark at all," Emmy pointed out coyly.

"Nice try," said Jesse.

Emmy pouted. "Oh, all right, I will wear the stinky thing," she said, lowering her long blue-green neck so Daisy could attach the leash to the collar.

Emmy set off, straining at the leash. Jesse and Daisy followed, Jesse holding the other end of the leash and Daisy beaming the flashlight ahead into the old mine tunnel.

They hadn't gotten very far when a deafening roar filled the air. The ground all around them began to rumble and shake. Up ahead, Emmy immediately transformed, collapsing into a quivering, whimpering heap of sheepdog.

Daisy turned to Jesse, her eyes wide with fear. "What's that?" she asked.

Over the noise, Jesse shouted, "It's the earth-mover!"

CHAPTER SIX

THE SKY IS FALLING!

The roaring noise stopped. The sound of their nervous breathing filled the silence. Jesse looked ahead into the tunnel, then behind them into the root cellar. The sun shone down into the hole, leaving a warm buttery patch at the foot of the stairs like a welcome mat. He signaled to the others to turn around and follow him back to the root cellar.

The three of them crowded into the patch of sunlight. Overhead, they heard a loud grinding of gears and brakes, then the earthmover's heavy door opened and clunked shut. They waited in tense silence for a few more minutes.

Jesse put his mouth to Daisy's ear and whispered, "Maybe he just parked it and went away."

She put her mouth to his ear and said, "Maybe he's waiting for us to come out so he can pounce on us and capture Emmy and . . ." *Drink Emmy's blood.* Daisy didn't want to say the last part aloud, not in front of Emmy.

But Jesse knew where she was going. He set his jaw. Very carefully and quietly, he climbed up the stairs and balanced himself on the door frame, straightening up just enough to see out over the edge of the hole. He didn't see anything. He didn't hear anything. He straightened up a little more.

The enormous orange earthmover stood right next to the barn, facing the Deep Woods, its front bumper mere feet from their hole. Jesse craned his neck. The cab seemed to be empty. He leaned down and signaled for Daisy and Emmy to join him.

"Look," he whispered to the others. "He's not in the cab. I don't know where he is, but if we crawl *under* the earthmover, we can sneak back to the rear . . . and then cut over and run for home. Plan?"

Daisy nodded and whispered, "Take off her leash."

Jesse unhitched the leash from Emmy's collar. Daisy turned around so Jesse could unzip the backpack. She switched off the flashlight and handed it to him.

When Jesse had finished tucking everything away and zipping up the backpack, he turned to Emmy and said, "Listen to me. This is very important."

Dog-form Emmy, panting, gave him her complete attention.

"Follow us. As soon as we get to the back end of the big orange machine, you run for it. But don't run until I tell you to. I'll hold up one finger, then two fingers. On the third finger, I want you to run as fast as you can. Head for the laurel bushes. Don't stop for anything, and don't look back. Wait for us there. I think you can. I think you can." He smiled encouragingly at Emmy, who let out two barely audible yips to show that she thought she could.

"Good girl," he whispered. Both cousins hugged the dog and pressed their faces into her fur, which smelled of damp dirt and a hint of hot chili peppers.

"We'll be right behind you," said Jesse.

Jesse eased himself up and out of the hole. He crawled over to the front bumper of the monstrous machine and then waited while the other two slithered up after him. Together they slipped under the machine. Jesse and Daisy ducked to avoid bumping their heads on the network of brand-new shiny ducts and pipes that ran down the center of the earthmover's giant underbelly. In a crouch they ran past enormous black treaded wheels. There were so many wheels that Jesse lost count by the time they reached the rear bumper and cleared it. There they stopped. Hands on knees, the cousins struggled to catch their breath. They were winded, as much from nerves as exertion. Emmy stood between them on her haunches, panting. Her eyes were on Jesse as she waited for the signal to run. Jesse crept over to the side of the earthmover and peered along the length of the vehicle. The coast looked clear.

Jesse held up one finger. Emmy's ears pricked up. Jesse held two fingers in front of him. Emmy stood and got ready. But as Jesse was about to raise the third finger, the earthmover's engine fired up, blasting them with boiling-hot diesel fumes.

"Run for it!" Jesse screamed.

Emmy exploded across the pasture and up the hill. Jesse and Daisy took off after her, but Jesse's shoelace got tangled in something. He sprawled face-first into a fat thistle plant. Jesse turned over, his face stinging with nettles and his head reeling. For a minute, he didn't even know where he was. Daisy tugged at his arm and pointed frantically at something. And then, as his senses returned, he saw the earthmover about to back over him. Its backing-up signal beeped ominously. Jesse rolled aside just in time to avoid being crushed beneath the giant rear wheels.

The earthmover continued to move in reverse until its massive body completely blocked their escape route.

"This way!" Daisy screamed. She took off toward the Deep Woods, the backpack slamming against her shoulder blades as she ran. Jesse scrambled to his feet and headed after her across the pasture. The earthmover was right behind them. It wasn't moving quickly, but fast enough for them to feel the massive metal scooper on the front bumper nipping at their heels. If one of them were to trip and fall, St. George would either scoop them up or run right over them.

As Jesse gaped at the dark wall of trees looming up before him, he had a sudden vision of St. George rolling into the Deep Woods, the earthmover leveling acres of trees as it churned after them. Jesse caught up with Daisy and pulled her off to the side. He dragged her, stumbling and staggering, around to the back end of the earthmover, where he shouted over the motor's thunder, "The door in the earth!"

Gasping for breath, with the sweat streaming down her face, Daisy nodded.

They took advantage of the time St. George needed to turn the earthmover around to rush back toward the barn. First Jesse and then Daisy leaped into the hole, bumped down the steps, and landed on their behinds on the root cellar floor.

"Safe!" screamed Daisy.

A great dark shadow loomed overhead, blocking out the sky. Jesse lunged for the backpack and unzipped it. He tossed the flashlight to Daisy and pulled out the ball of string. Quickly, he tied one end of the string to a stanchion of the canning shelves, just as dirt began pouring down on their heads.

He looked around frantically for Daisy, but she was already waiting for him at the entrance to the mine tunnel, beaming her flashlight like a beacon. He reached her and spun around. They both watched as a cascade of rocks and earth poured into the root cellar, flowing toward the tunnel.

Emmy's voice, like a golden bell, rang in Jesse's

head: *The sky is falling! Run, Chicken Little! Run!*

Daisy shouted over the noise of the churning earthmover. "Where's Emmy?"

Jesse shouted back, "The laurel bushes!"

There was an alarming series of muffled explosions. Then there was silence. Dirt now covered the mineshaft entrance completely.

Daisy's face looked ghostly and grim in the flashlight's beam. "Well, that's that, I guess," she said.

"Maybe Emmy will come back with the magic shovel and dig us out," Jesse said.

"Then shouldn't we stick around?" Daisy asked.

"I'm worried that the mine might keep collapsing. I think we need to get away from this spot for now," Jesse said. "Besides, if my hunch is right, this tunnel winds up beneath the Deep Woods clearing."

Daisy didn't want to say that if Jesse's hunch was right, then St. George had them trapped either way. So she shut her mouth and turned to lead the way into the tunnel. Jesse followed, unraveling string from the big ball as he went. Daisy was a little surprised that she wasn't *more* terrified. Maybe she was too thankful to be afraid; thankful that St. George hadn't squished them flat with the earthmover, that Emmy had made it safely to the laurel bushes, that Jesse was with her and she wasn't alone.

As she walked, she shone the flashlight all around even though there really wasn't very much to see. The tunnel was framed with wood that looked very old and alarmingly rotten in places. Long, hairy tree roots reached down through the ceiling. Daisy and Jesse had to duck to avoid getting tangled in them.

"We're under the Deep Woods now," Jesse said with certainty.

"At least we're going in the right direction," Daisy said brightly.

"Yep," said Jesse.

Every so often, other tunnels branched out to either side, but the cousins stuck to what felt like the main tunnel. Without a compass, there was no real telling if they were going in the right direction or not.

Daisy was the first to break a long silence. "Sure is dark down here," she said.

"Sure is," said Jesse.

"I don't know about you, but I don't think I've ever been in darkness quite this . . . deep."

"It's pretty deep, all right."

Then they lapsed back into silence. Daisy did not want to say aloud the other thoughts that were streaming through her brain. What if St. George had captured Emmy? What if this mine didn't connect to the one St. George was working in? This area was honeycombed with old mines, but they didn't necessarily all link up into one big network. What if the one way out of this place was now completely sealed?

They plodded on, their mouths dry, but neither wanting to stop and drink, not with the darkness swarming just beyond the flashlight's feeble beam like something alive.

After a while, Daisy let out a yelp. There was a small thud, two bright flashes, and then a darkness that was so complete, it was as if they had both suddenly gone blind.

"Daisy!" Jesse crept forward. "Where are you? What happened? Are you okay?"

"I'm okay," she said after a beat. Her voice came from farther away than he expected. "My hair got snagged in one of those tree roots and I . . . oh, Jess, I needed both hands to get my hair loose and I—I dropped the flashlight."

"Where?" Jesse asked.

"Over here, I think," she said.

"Keep talking so I can find you," Jesse said.

Daisy prattled, "I hate my hair. My bandanna must have fallen off when we were running. If I

ever get out of here, I'm going to shave it all off
and—"

"Got you!" Jesse said, fastening his hand
around one slender wrist.

She clutched at him. "Jesse, we have to stick
together."

"Of course we do," he said. He could tell she
was so scared that there was no room for him to be.
"Hold on to my belt loops in back," he told her.
"We'll work our way up and down a ways. The flashlight's got to be close by. I'm going to get on my
hands and knees, so you have to come with me.
Okay, Daze?"

"Whatever you say," she said shakily.

He got down and groped around in the dirt,
towing Daisy behind him.

Daisy tapped him on the right arm and said,
"Try over there!"

Then, with a jolt, Jesse realized that they had
lost something just as important as the flashlight:
the ball of string. He must have let go of it when he
heard Daisy cry out.

"We lost the string, too, didn't we?" Daisy said
in a sad little voice. When Jesse didn't answer, she
wailed, "I knew it! It's all my fault."

"No, it's not," he said.

He lay back in the soft dirt and Daisy went with

him. She was sobbing. He wanted to open his mouth and bawl like a baby right along with her, but he told himself it would only make both of them feel worse.

We should have stayed and waited, he thought. Why had he led them into the old mine? It was the stupidest idea he'd ever had. Why had Daisy followed along? She knew better. Now no one would ever be able to find them. They were as good as buried alive. And, as if all that weren't bad enough, Jesse had to pee.

If this is a magical adventure, then I want my old life back.

"I am so, so sorry," Daisy said, letting out a huge shuddering yawn. She mumbled, "I should have put you in charge of the flashlight, and now it's all my fault that we're lost. And I *hate* my hair."

"It's not your fault or your hair's fault, either, okay, Daisy?"

"Okay," she said. After a short silence, she asked, "Are you hungry? I'm starved. I could eat a giant pizza burger with double fries right now."

Jesse smiled in the darkness. "How about an energy bar instead?"

"I'll take it," she said.

"Hand me the backpack," he said.

"Here," she said.

Jesse fumbled for the zipper. He unzipped it and reached around inside. His fingers grazed the jar of worms and for one wild moment, he thought they might be saved. Then he remembered Miss Alodie's directions to use them only in the presence of the book. The next thing he felt (and smelled!) was Emmy's head of cabbage. He was just about to toss it when he thought: *We might wind up eating it if we get desperate.* Jesse shuddered. His fingers lit gratefully upon an energy bar.

"Here," he said, holding it out. Daisy snatched it from his fingers.

"Thanks," she said. He heard the crackle of paper as she tore it open. Then he heard her take a bite and chew.

He crawled off a little ways and relieved himself. Following the sound of her chewing, he returned to the backpack and found another energy bar, tore it open, and ate it greedily.

After that, they both fell asleep with their heads on the backpack, even though the cabbage and the jar of worms made it a far from ideal pillow.

A light woke up Jesse, flickering on the insides of his eyelids, pink as the first blush of dawn. He opened his eyes and blinked while beside him, Daisy also began to stir.

A band of hobgoblins with torches stood around them in a circle, staring at them with eyes that were without pupils or irises, red-rimmed and milky white.

Daisy squeezed Jesse's wrist. A noise rose up from the hobgoblins, a dark, moist, grunting and snuffling through their snouts. It was a very *underground* sound.

Jesse counted seven of them. Three had bamboo torches, the kind you buy in a garden store. Tiki torches. The other four had sharp pickaxes hoisted over their shoulders. The cuffs of their orange jumpsuits dragged in the dirt. One of them had rolled up the cuffs of his pants, and Daisy nearly cried out when she saw his feet. His feet were bare and *he had no toes*! Where his toes were supposed to be was just a grayish wedge.

"Let's see who we've got here," said Jesse. "Sleepy, Dopey, Dumpy, Grubby . . ."

"Jess, this isn't funny!" Daisy whispered. "It's— it's—" She fumbled for the right word. *"Hideous!"*

But Jesse couldn't help himself. Now he understood why heroes in action movies made dumb jokes when they were in trouble. They did it to keep from screaming their heads off. "What do you want?" Jesse asked the hobgoblins, in what he hoped was a stern, steady he-man voice.

He got more snuffling in reply. Daisy said, "Jess, they might not use words, like us."

One of them sidled over on his bandy legs and pulled Jesse to his feet. Daisy, hanging on to Jesse's belt loop, came up with him. The hobgoblins crowded in closer and stared. One of them thrust out his mittenlike hand to Daisy. He was holding her purple bandanna.

"I think he wants you to take it," said Jesse.

Daisy shot out a trembling hand and snatched the bandanna away from the hobgoblin. "Thanks," she said, forcing a polite smile and hastily tying the bandanna around her head.

Another hobgoblin offered Jesse the lost flashlight, and still another of the odd creatures held out the ball of string.

"Thanks, guys," Jesse said as he took the flashlight from the one hobgoblin and the ball of string from the other. He moved in slow motion as he bent down and unzipped the backpack, put the stuff away, zipped up the backpack, straightened, and slipped the backpack straps around his shoulders. The hobgoblins' eyes followed his every move with utter fascination.

"Do you think we look as weird and scary to

them as they do to us?" Jesse wondered aloud.

"If you ask me, they look even scarier up close," said Daisy warily.

"I don't know," Jesse said thoughtfully, "I was just thinking that they seem a little less scary now. See how they're looking at us? They don't look mean at all. In fact—"

Daisy cried out, "Look! They're crying! Ohmygosh, Jess! The hobgoblins are *crying*."

"Their tears . . . they're actually muddy," Jesse said. Although pretty much everything about the hobgoblins was muddy, there was something about those muddy brown tears that not only moved Jesse's heart but also his brain.

"I think I know what they are," he said quietly. "I mean, besides hobgoblins and chthonic ones and St. George's minions. Daisy, these are the children of the earth the professor was talking about. We're looking right at them. *St. George's first victims.*"

Daisy, who had begun to think the exact same thing, said, "They are, aren't they?"

The hobgoblins prodded them gently with their mitts and they began to move forward as a group.

"And you know what else?" Daisy said as they marched along the tunnel with their hobgoblin escorts. "I think they brought those torches for us."

Jesse nodded. "Probably they see fine in the dark," he said. "Or sense things . . . like bats."

At the mention of bats, Daisy reached up and patted the bandanna on her head. "That would make sense," she said. "Do you think they're taking us to St. George?"

"Probably," said Jesse. "But it's not their fault, Daze. What choice do they have? St. George has made them his slaves, right?"

"Poor things. They probably don't like St. George any more than we do," she said. Somehow it made Daisy feel better to have been taken captive by beings who were themselves captives. "Well, at least he didn't catch Emmy in his trap. She's safe in the laurel bushes."

"Right," said Jesse, but he wished he knew that for sure.

They soon arrived at a spot where several tunnels came together to form a star. A massive tree root grew right down the center of it. The hobgoblins halted before the root. For one uneasy moment, Daisy was afraid that the root might be blocking the way. But then the hobgoblins arranged themselves around the tree root and sat cross-legged, like kids at circle time. They looked up at Jesse and Daisy and made that moist, grunting, earthy sound again.

"What do you guys want?" Jesse asked them.

"Maybe they want us to admire the humongous tree root," said Daisy. "But I've kind of had enough tree roots for the time being, thank you very much."

Still, even Daisy had to admit that it was an impressive sight, this hairy, densely tangled network of roots that hung down in a ball almost to the floor.

They were startled when the very next moment, they heard a deep voice coming from inside the tree root: "You may approach Her Eminence!"

CHAPTER SEVEN

HER ROYAL LOWNESS

The voice coming out of the tree root sounded like a bullfrog, if bullfrogs could do more than belch.

Jesse and Daisy exchanged looks of surprise. "Another talking tree?" Jesse whispered.

Daisy frowned. She wasn't so sure. She wasn't exactly an expert, but it didn't *sound* like a dryad.

The hobgoblins shifted to clear a path for their guests. Jesse and Daisy approached the strange tree root cautiously.

Daisy peered into the tangle of hairy tendrils and thought she saw a pair of shiny eyes staring back at her. Perhaps it was a dryad after all.

"You find yourselves staring into the magnificent eyes—which we have *not* given you permission to do—of Queen Hap of the Hobgoblin Hive of Hobhorn," said the froggy voice.

"What's a hobhorn?" Jesse wanted to know.

"It is our mountain home," the queen said.

"You mean Old Mother Mountain?" Daisy asked.

"*You* might mean Old Mother Mountain," said the queen distastefully. "But it's the Hobhorn to us, and always has been, and we would know, wouldn't we? Now, hold your tongues and go down on your knees before us!"

Jesse and Daisy each went awkwardly down on one knee. The hobgoblins scrambled down onto both knees and put their foreheads to the ground. Daisy looked over and shook her head at Jesse. "No way," she whispered.

"As you were!" croaked the queen.

Jesse and Daisy climbed to their feet again.

"How do you do?" Jesse said politely.

Daisy blurted, "If you're a queen, what are you doing inside some dirty old root-ball?"

The queen bellowed, "We have not given you permission to address us!"

Daisy rolled her eyes and mimed zipping her lips.

"But to answer the question, nevertheless," said the queen, "which, we might add, is most astute, we are prisoners and this foul ball of fibrous cellulose is our jaily-waily."

"Jaily-waily?" Jesse mouthed.

Daisy had to cover her mouth to keep from giggling.

"We find ourselves in a uniquely helpless, not to say hapless, situation," the queen said huffily.

Daisy and Jesse bobbed their heads in silent sympathy.

After a pause, the queen snapped, "Oh, very well, you may address Her Eminence."

Jesse went first. "Did St. George put you—eh, Your Eminence—in there?" he asked.

"Good guess!" she croaked. "So far we have one good question and one good guess. That's a better score than most Upper Realmers could earn."

Daisy moved even closer to the ball and stared

into the riot of roots. Sure enough, in the very center of the root-ball, a hobgoblin squatted on her haunches. She looked just like her subjects, except that she was softer and rounder-looking, with big moss-green eyes (which really *were* magnificent!) and reddish hair with a bit of curl to it. Instead of the orange jumpsuit, she wore a robe decorated with tiny snail shells. Daisy had never thought of brown as being a pretty color for a garment, but this was the most beautiful hue of brown that Daisy had ever seen. It reminded her of fresh dirt with a hint of glittering mica in it.

"Hey there, Your Royal Highness," Daisy said softly.

"That's Royal *Lowness* to you," the queen corrected snappishly.

Jesse poked his nose into the roots next to Daisy and asked, "What's wrong with *Highness*?"

"*High-ness*," said Her Majesty testily, "like *lightness*, is overrated by you Upper Realm types."

"I see," said Jesse, having never thought of himself as an Upper Realm *type*. "I guess that makes sense . . . to a hobgoblin brain."

"How did St. George catch Your Lowness?" Daisy wanted to know.

"He tricked us," the queen said with a heavy

sigh. "Not that we didn't, unfortunately, make it easy for him. He spun us that same old tired tale. 'A treasure of untold vastness lies just beneath your hive.' And to think that we fell for it! If we helped him find it, he promised to go halvsies. He led us here on a wild treasure chase and before you could say 'Hob's your uncle!' we were stuck in here. Now the hive has no leader. Most of our subjects have fallen in line behind St. George . . . except for this small faithful band of rebels you see here."

The rebel hobgoblins grunted earthily and raised their mitts and torches in a show of unity.

"St. George has the rest of them digging for the treasure," the queen said. "Our hobbies, our rough little gems of the earth, are nothing but free labor to that villainous swine."

Jesse nodded. "We've seen your hobbies at work. Digging in the clearing . . . in the Deep Woods."

"Greedy rapscallion that he is, St. George wants the treasure all to himself. But we know, now that our hob head's screwed back on tightly, that the treasure he seeks isn't meant for the likes of him, or even for us. It belongs . . . to the *draggy-wagons*."

"The dragons, you mean?" said Jesse.

Her Lowness nodded.

"Well, it happens that the two of us are Dragon Keepers," said Daisy.

"Are you, now?" The hobgoblin queen gave them a shrewd look. "Then where are you keeping your draggy-wagon?"

"We got split up from our draggy-wagon," Daisy said carefully. She was feeling a tad defensive, so she changed the subject quickly. "Can we help Your Lowness escape? Maybe use your hobgoblins' picks to break up this root-ball?"

Her Lowness shook her head. "That won't work. The tree holds us fast. St. George has spelled it. He's enslaved all of the trees. The trees were the first to fall under his power . . . weak, spindly suckers of the light and the water that they are. Then, owing to our own foolishness, the hobgoblins were the next. Not that it took much. Except for Yours Truly, hobgoblins are followers, not leaders. But who's next? That's what we ask ourselves as we sit here fretting in our royal dungeon. St. George is a blight upon the very earth, we tell you. A blight."

"Where did he come from?" Jesse asked.

"Who knows?" said the queen with a shrug of her plump shoulders. "Where does anything come from? He's been on this earth for ages. He lives off the draggy-wagons, that one, and he always has. He's a parasite. You know the old nursery rhyme: 'Georgie Porgie, pudding and pie, killed the draggy-wagons and made them cry.'"

Jesse and Daisy stared at each other blankly. That certainly wasn't the version of the nursery rhyme *they* had grown up with!

The queen went on. "He goes in cycles. After he's slain the dragons into near-extinction, he sleeps. He just woke up a short while ago from a long sleep in the collapsed mine shaft."

"How did he get out?" Daisy asked.

"We couldn't rightly say," said the queen. "We've been asleep ourselves. When there are no dragons alive in the world, there is no magic. When there is no magic, we ethereal beings either sleep or fade away. You might not know it to look at us," she said haughtily, "but we are Beings of the Ethereal Plain."

"I'm sure we—I mean, Your Lowness—is," Daisy said.

Jesse, who had been listening closely, said, "Maybe somebody dug him up by accident."

"I doubt it," said the queen. "Our theory is that he sensed the arrival of a new draggy-wagon— namely, yours—and he just worked his way up out of the earth, like a sliver of glass out of a finger. You have but to set us free and we will turn the tide of this battle. We won't lay a mitt on your treasure, either; you have our royal word on that."

"Yes, but how do we get you out of there?" Daisy said.

"We thought you'd never ask!" said Her Royal Lowness. "You must fetch us the Golden Pickax."

"Right," said Jesse. "Just tell us where it is and we'll get it for you."

"Oh, we can't help you there," said Her Lowness.

"But it could be *anywhere*," said Jesse.

"Not *anywhere*." The queen shook her head and croaked, "If it was somewhere down here, we would have found it already."

"Is Your Lowness a hundred percent sure?" Daisy asked. "Sometimes I think I've lost something and it winds up being right under my nose. What about these pickaxes here?" she said, pointing to the ones resting across the hobgoblins' laps. "Could any of these be the Golden Pickax . . . I mean, in disguise?" she added doubtfully, because they certainly didn't look like they were made of gold.

"No," said the queen. "It's in the Upper Realm, somewhere nearby, I'm sure. The Upper Realm is your turf. We're sure you know where everything is and can locate it easily. Now hop to it, lambies, for Queen Hap, will you?"

Feeling nowhere near as confident in their ability to find the Golden Pickax as Her Royal Lowness was, Jesse and Daisy bid the queen farewell, promising only to do their best. The hobgoblin band hopped to its feet and led the cousins down one of the tunnels radiating out from the queen's root-ball prison.

"Do you think the professor will have some ideas?" Daisy asked as they jogged to keep up with the hobgoblins.

"Probably not," said Jesse. "Pickaxes are mining tools. Remember, he is a dragon man, not a mine man."

"What about Miss Alodie?" Daisy said.

"I have a feeling that the next time she wants to see us is with the book," said Jesse.

"The book! I forgot all about that," said Daisy worriedly. "We haven't used the earthworms yet."

"Why would we even need to?" Jesse asked. "There must be millions of them down here."

"I sure hope these guys are taking us to the exit and not straight to St. George," Daisy said.

"The queen said they are her loyal band of rebels," said Jesse in a queenly croak.

"Yeah, but didn't she also say that hobgoblins

are followers? Maybe once they get away from the queen, they fall back under Georgie Porgie's power," said Daisy.

"Don't ask me why, but I trust them," said Jesse.

"Me too," said Daisy. "In fact, I think the hobbies are adorable."

Jesse smiled. "We used to think they were hideous. Now we think they're adorable," he said. "I think that's kind of cool."

Just then, the hobgoblins halted and spit on their palms, extinguishing their torches with their bare hands. Jesse and Daisy winced. But after the torches were snuffed out, the tunnel was still light.

"We must be near an exit," said Daisy, lowering her voice to a whisper.

In a few moments, the tunnel opened out into an underground cavern. It looked natural, rather than man-made, and it was enormous, as big as a cathedral. Natural light shone down through a hole in the ceiling. A wide wooden ramp led up to it. More tunnels, at least a dozen of them, pocked the cavern walls. Except for Jesse and Daisy and the band of rebels, the cavern seemed to be deserted. But from somewhere, perhaps down one of the other tunnels, came the distinctive ring of metal on stone. The hobgoblins were hard at work doing their new master's bidding.

One of the hobgoblins ran into the middle of the cavern and came to a stop beside a throne made of stone and studded with snail shells and black pearls.

"That must be the throne of Her Royal Lowness," Daisy said.

Another hobgoblin plucked Jesse's sleeve and pointed to the ramp, making a shooing motion. Then he hurried over to the base of the ramp and beckoned them forward with both mitts.

Jesse and Daisy ran halfway up the ramp. Then, Jesse caught a glimpse of something dark red underneath the ramp. He grabbed Daisy's arm and pointed. "Look," he said. "The book."

They hurried back down the ramp and ducked under it. The big book lay crosswise on top of a stout wooden wagon. It looked bigger than ever, bigger than a grand front door in some palace, with the indecipherable gold markings on the cover making it ever so mysterious.

Daisy said, "Why would he bring it down here? This can't be a very good place for a valuable old book like this."

"Nope, but I bet he has a good reason," Jesse said, walking toward the book with his hand outstretched. He just wanted to touch it again, and then they could go. About two feet from the book, his knuckles struck something. He flexed his hand and stared before him. Nothing was there, no obstructions that he could see.

Daisy came up beside him with both hands outstretched. Her hands met and then flattened against a surface that was completely unseen and yet obviously solid. She leaned her full weight against the invisible wall, but she could neither budge it nor get any closer to the book.

The hobgoblins gathered round and snuffled curiously.

Jesse followed the invisible wall with his hands, looking for a gap or a chink, but it continued clear around the book, and he eventually wound up back where he had started. When Jesse rubbed his hand against the wall, it made the squeaking sound a balloon makes when you've blown it up too big.

"Try to pop it," Daisy suggested.

Jesse hauled off and punched the wall, but his fist came back and punched him equally hard in the face. "Ouch!" Jesse said, cupping his nose in both hands.

The hobgoblins thought this was very funny. They snorted and snickered and pointed their mitts at him.

Jesse and Daisy turned around and leaned their backs against the wall.

"Don't you feel like one of those obnoxious mimes?" Daisy said.

"Reminds me of the invisible fence Aunt Maggie put up to keep Emmy in," Jesse said.

"Except this one squeaks instead of zaps," said Daisy.

"And punches," Jesse added, rubbing his nose. Then he turned around thoughtfully and leaned his forehead and palms against the invisible wall, as if he were staring at a tantalizing display in a store window. He had another thought. "Daze, open the backpack. Get the worms."

"No, Jess. Now isn't the time," Daisy said. "It's time to get out of here."

The hobgoblins seemed to agree with Daisy. They gestured toward the ramp. One of them was jabbing his mitt in the direction of the tunnel, where the hammering was going on, shaking his head in a worried fashion.

"Just a second, fellas," Jesse said to the hobgoblins, and then to Daisy, "Miss Alodie said we're supposed to let the worms out when we are in the presence of the big book."

"Yeah, but she also said we'd know when the moment was right. She said it would hit us. I'm not feeling hit. All I'm feeling is we need to get the Sam Hill out of here."

The hobgoblins snorted sharply and bobbed their heads in agreement.

Jesse sighed and pushed himself away from the wall. "It's not the right time, I guess. Let's get out of here."

As Jesse and Daisy walked up the ramp, the rebel hobgoblins stood below and waved good-bye to them with their mitts. Daisy heard a gurgling sound behind her and looked back. One of the hobgoblins was crying fat muddy tears. He blew his snout hard on the sleeve of his jumpsuit and blubbered softly.

Daisy went back down the ramp. She took the bandanna off her head and mimed blowing her nose into it. "Here," she said, tucking it into the hobgoblin's jumpsuit sleeve. "Use it in good health." Then, running up the ramp, she joined Jesse in the Upper Realm.

At the top of the ramp, the cousins stepped into the middle of the clearing in the Deep Woods, just as Jesse had suspected they would. Daisy let herself stand there for a few seconds, head thrown back, taking in big deep breaths of sweet, fresh air.

Jesse did the same, then raised his wrist and looked at his watch. He tapped the face to make sure it was working. "Holy moly, Daze, it's almost seven-thirty!" he said, looking around.

"So we're an hour late for dinner," she said. "We can talk our way out of that kind of trouble any day. We'll just say your watch stopped."

Jesse shook his head, feeling suddenly exhausted. "Daze, it's seven-thirty *in the morning*. See where the sun is? It's *rising,* not *setting*. We've been underground *all night long*."

Daisy's jaw dropped. "Yikes!" she cried out. "We are in so much *trouble!*"

They racewalked down the path away from the clearing in the Deep Woods, but it was hard going. Now that Jesse and Daisy knew they had been out all night, their heads swam, their limbs felt as if they were filled with wet concrete, and their eyelids felt scratchy as sandpaper. In the gathering light, they staggered across the pasture. They stopped for a moment to shake their heads at the deep muddy grooves the earthmover had left, and at the patch of tread-flattened dirt where the hole to the root cellar and the old mine tunnel had been.

"Maybe we should check the barn and make sure the Magic Museum's okay," Jesse said nervously.

"We have to get home!" Daisy said. "We have to find Emmy."

At this, Emmy burst out of the laurel bushes and came running down the hill to meet them.

"My Keepers!" she cried. "I was so sad and scared. But I stayed in the bushes and waited and waited for you just like you told me to." She grabbed them in a great big dragon hug.

"You are a very good dragon," said Daisy, laughing with relief.

"And you are very good Keepers, because you came back for me," said Emmy, setting them down gently. "My friends said you would come back, and you did."

"So did the dryads keep you company?" Jesse asked.

"Alllll night long. I was scared. The laurel dryads were plotting against me. They wanted to hand me over to the Slayer. Nasty laurel *wenches*!" Emmy said, pouting.

"It's not their fault," said Daisy. "They're St. George's slaves."

"My friends came and told those wicked wenches to hold their traitorous tongues. Then Douglas and the lady brought me lots and lots of dandelion greens, and I ate so much that I am full, full, full. And now I need my cozy nest of socks, please, thank you, you're welcome, much obliged, you're too, *too* kind."

Emmy turned around and ran back up the hill, diving into the laurels. Crawling behind her, the

cousins watched as her long dragon tail transformed into the furry little nub of a sheepdog.

Jesse and Daisy and their faithful dog trudged
into the backyard toward home. Daisy thought that
her house had never looked quite so peaceful and
inviting. The lights in the kitchen were on and the
windows were fogged up. Then she thought of her
parents waiting inside and suddenly she didn't feel
quite so welcome anymore. They would be drinking
their umpteenth cup of coffee, drumming their fingers on the kitchen table. Had they called the police? How much money, she wondered, had they
put up for information leading to their return?

Jesse hurriedly unlocked the garage door and
watched as Emmy scampered over to her nest in
the packing crate, leaped in, and burrowed under
the socks. Then he locked the door and turned to
Daisy. "Okay," he said, breathing deeply to calm his
nerves. "What's our story?" Dealing with your own
angry parents is bad enough. Dealing with someone
else's angry parents was petrifying.

Daisy said in a voice like iron, "When all else
fails . . . the truth—sort of: that we got lost in the
Deep Woods and we're really, *really* sorry and we'll
never do it again, and maybe they'll be so glad we
didn't get torn apart by bears and wolverines, they
won't ground us for the rest of time." She took a

deep breath and marched up the back stairs into the house.

When she saw her parents sitting at the kitchen table, Daisy realized with a sickening jolt that she hadn't seen them since breakfast the morning before. But Aunt Maggie looked up from her newspaper and smiled with unnatural brightness.

"Hey, kids," she said. "You're home early. Did you have fun?"

CHAPTER EIGHT

THE MAGICAL DAIRYMAN

Jesse and Daisy turned to each other and blinked once. Home early?

Daisy, shrugging, turned back to her mother. "We had a great time, didn't we, Jess?" She gave him a sharp elbow to the ribs.

Jesse nodded so hard, it rattled his brains against his skull.

"How is Miss Alodie doing?" Uncle Joe asked in a strange flat voice neither of the cousins had ever heard him use before.

"She's great," Jesse said, staring curiously at his uncle.

"It's her ankle I'm talking about," Uncle Joe droned. "Tell us. Is her ankle better?"

"Oh, her *ankle!*" Daisy said, digging her nails into Jesse's palm. "Much better. Right? It's much better," she prompted Jesse.

"Better," Jesse echoed dumbly, and then he caught on. "Oh, her *ankle!* It's, um, good!"

"That's good," said Uncle Joe, nodding mechanically. "She called to tell us about it yesterday afternoon. I offered to take her to the clinic. But she said if the cousins could stay and help her keep off the ankle, all would be well."

"Yes, indeedy!" Aunt Maggie said with scary intensity. "Keeping a sprained ankle elevated is very, very, very, very important!"

"Don't worry," said Daisy doubtfully. "Everything's fine."

Then Aunt Maggie gave her head a quick shake and looked at Jesse and Daisy as if she were seeing them for the first time. "Really? That's good! But how did you two get so *grubby*?" she asked. "You look like you spent the night with the hobgoblins in the coal mines."

Jesse was so sure his hair was standing on end that he actually reached up to smooth it flat.

"We were up late weeding," said Daisy. "Miss Alodie said it works best . . . by moonlight."

"That woman's a real character," said Aunt Maggie with a fond shake of her head. "Go grab yourselves a hot shower. Are you hungry? You look hungry."

"We are!" said Daisy. "We fixed some . . . porridge and nuts and dried fruit for Miss Alodie, but you know how I feel about porridge."

Uncle Joe's face dissolved into a familiar goofy grin. "Remember we used to call it mush, Daze?" he asked. "Daisy never could stomach porridge, even when she was a baby. I remember you used to spit it out clear across the kitchen. Olympic-class projectile vomiting."

Daisy and Jesse grinned wearily at each other, remembering Emmy's own mush-spewing phase not so very long ago.

"I'll fry you up a mess of eggs and sausage," said Uncle Joe.

"Thanks, Poppy. We promised we'd go back to Miss Alodie's later, didn't we, Jess? She, um, needs us to fix dinner for her." Daisy gave Jesse another elbow jab.

"Yeah," said Jesse. "She also needs us to get her a book. A nice big one."

"That'll keep her off the ankle," said Uncle Joe.

"You know," said Aunt Maggie, "I think it's great that Miss Alodie has such considerate neighbors to help her out in a fix."

Jesse and Daisy, nodding quickly, eased themselves out the door into the hallway. On the way up the stairs, Daisy whispered to Jesse, "Miss Alodie must have put some sort of spell on my parents, don't you think?"

"Maybe," Jesse whispered back. "But sometimes parents can go weird like that all on their own."

"That's true," said Daisy.

After showering and changing into clean clothes, then polishing off three eggs, three sausages, and three English muffins between them, the cousins went back upstairs to visit the professor online. Whether he would be able to help them or not, they still wanted to tell a grown-up about everything that had happened to them in the past twenty-four hours.

As soon as his familiar face appeared on the screen, Jesse and Daisy leaned forward eagerly and started telling him about the door in the earth and all that had happened to them since they had gone through it. The professor listened, leaning back and stroking his beard. At the mention of the Golden Pickax, he sat upright and said, "Now *that* I can help you with. It's on the barn wall, where I left it, hidden in plain sight among my own tools."

Jesse smacked the desk and rolled backward, pointing an accusatory finger at the computer screen. "You!" he whispered. "You're the farmer!"

"The Magical Dairyman," said Daisy in a voice of awe.

Daisy and Jesse looked at each other and laughed. Then Daisy turned back to the screen and said, "We thought we had made you up! But you're real."

"In a manner of speaking, yes," said the professor. "I have been many things and led many lives, and dairy farmer was, indeed, one of them."

"So let me see if I've got this right," Jesse said. "You were the farmer and St. George was pretending to work for the mining company so he could dig up the dragon treasure."

"Good sleuthing!" said the professor, beaming.

Daisy asked, "So now he's going after the treasure again?"

"It's far more valuable and far more important

than a mere treasure. But waste no more time in conversation with me. You must get the Golden Pickax without delay and keep it out of St. George's clutches. With the Golden Pickax he will be able to reach the treasure with ease. *The pickax knows where to dig.* Much hangs on your actions, Dragon Keepers, so tread very carefully."

Jesse turned to Daisy. "I guess we have to wake up Emmy," he said.

At that, the backdrop behind Professor Andersson burst into a wall of red-hot roiling flames. The professor leaned forward, the flames reflecting in his eyes. He opened his mouth and bellowed at them, "LEAVE THE DRAGON IN HER LAIR AND GO ON ALONE!"

Then the screen hissed into blackness.

The cousins sat in stunned silence.

Then Jesse said, "That guy sure is dramatic."

"I guess we have to do like he says and let Emmy sleep," said Daisy. She rubbed her face. "I'm so tired, I could sleep for a hundred years myself."

"Me too," said Jesse. "But we can't sleep yet. We've got Dragon Keeper business to do."

Jesse went to the mudroom and got their backpack. He checked the jar to make sure that the worms were still alive (they were quite lively!). Then he tossed out the head of cabbage (which was *really* stinky!), changed the water in their canteen, and packed up a couple of sandwiches. Daisy went to the living room and told Aunt Maggie that they were going first to the Dell, then to the library, and later to Miss Alodie's for dinner.

"Okay," Aunt Maggie said, "but try to be home for an early-ish bedtime. You look tired, both of you."

On their way past the Rock Shop, Uncle Joe shouted through the screen window. "Hey, guys! I just remembered the farmer's name. It was Lukas Burton Andersson!"

"We know!" the cousins shot back as they ran up the rise toward the Dell. Coming down the hill from the laurel bushes, Daisy tried to picture the wall of the barn and the rusty old tools that had been hanging there for decades. Was the pickax still there?

When they got to the barn, they stood and scanned the wall above their Magic Museum. The magic shovel was hanging back in its spot, but just above it and slightly to the right was a perfect pickax-shaped silhouette on the wall where the red paint was less faded.

"It was hanging right *there*," Daisy said, jabbing her finger at the spot.

Jesse sat down hard on the milking stool and

buried his head in his arms. *"That's* what he was doing here yesterday. He ran us out of the way so he could come in here and get the pickax."

"Because," said Daisy, "the Golden Pickax knows where to dig."

"It knows where to dig up the dragon treasure," said Jesse.

"Don't call it a treasure," Daisy reminded him.

"The Important and Valuable Thing," Jesse said, lifting his head wearily.

"He probably took it to the cavern. The cavern is his new headquarters," said Daisy. "We're going to have to sneak in there and steal it. Everything hangs on our keeping the Golden Pickax out of his clutches."

"How are we going to do that?" Jesse asked.

"I don't know, just be really sneaky, I guess," Daisy said. "Maybe he's asleep."

"Maybe . . . ," said Jesse. "But maybe he's wide awake and ready for us."

"I've been thinking," Daisy said, "about that ramp. It's about fifteen or so feet off the ground of the cavern when you first go in, wouldn't you say?"

"Yeah, about," said Jesse.

"So maybe we can lower ourselves over the side and drop down beneath the ramp, where the big book is. We'll hide there and wait for our chance," said Daisy.

"That could work," said Jesse, "unless he happens to be doing something with the book."

"The ramp has gaps between the boards," said Daisy. "We can peek down and check first."

"Okay," Jesse said with a sigh. "Let's go."

They went across the pasture. Just as they were entering the Deep Woods, the dryads drifted out of their tree trunks and stood before them. Their forms were even paler in broad daylight. In fact, if you didn't already know what they looked like, you might not be able to see them at all. Only the sashes Miss Alodie had given them were truly visible, floating in the air about six feet off the ground.

"Thanks for dragon-sitting," Daisy said to them.

"It was our d-d-d-duty and our p-p-p-pleasure," said Lady Aspen.

"Could you spare us a moment of your time?" asked Douglas Fir.

"We'd like to, but we can't," said Jesse. "We're here on Dragon Keeper business and it really can't wait."

"S-s-s-someone has heard about you and w-w-w-wants to meet you," said Lady Aspen.

"It won't take a minute, we promise," said Douglas Fir.

The cousins reluctantly followed the ghostlike forms of the dryads as they slipped across the pasture to where a big old willow tree grew beside the brook. The cousins knew the tree well. When they were little, it was their pretend castle, but when they got older, they played mostly in the barn.

As they drew nearer to the tree, they heard a low wailing sound, like the wind in the willow, only louder and sharper. The sound soon resolved itself into words. "Oh, good grief! Here they come. Oh, no, this is terrible. What will they think of me?"

"There, now, old fellow, it's not so bad. Help is on the way!" Douglas Fir said in a soft, kindly voice. "Look here, we've brought the children with us so you can see them with your own eyes."

There, in the gnarled trunk of the willow tree, Jesse and Daisy saw a creature that seemed arrested midway between dryad and solid tree form. Its mouth was a jagged crack running across the bark of the lower trunk. Its large drooping knothole eyes, set just above the mouth, streamed with tears. "Go away! Go away!" he sobbed, as he shook loose hanks of green willow hair from his head and mopped his wet cheeks.

"Willow, please," said Douglas Fir. "Can't you

stop weeping at least long enough to say hello to Jesse and Daisy?"

"Hi," said Jesse and Daisy awkwardly.

The willow hid his face behind two lower branches and howled, "Oh, no! Go away! Don't look at me! Not now, please! I'm a wreck. I'm a pathetic mess. My leaves are a shambles, my bark is sodden, and I'm in no shape to entertain guests. I'm miserable, can't you see?" And he fell into another fit of weeping.

"I get it," Jesse said to Daisy. "This is the tree that's holding the hobgoblin queen captive underground in his roots."

"Right!" said Daisy. "Of course!"

Douglas and Lady Aspen both nodded their leafy heads in confirmation.

"Oh, sure, blame the victim!" said the willow. "It's all *my* fault! But it's that wretched St. George who's to blame. I have no power. I'm nothing but a miserable weak wreck of a weeping willow. Do you think I *asked* to have my root-ball inhabited by a hobgoblin? I don't care if she is the queen! Do you know what it feels like to be *infested*?" He shuddered and wept with his branches heaving and long pale green wisps drifting to the earth like ticker tape at the world's saddest parade.

"Gee, that's terrible," said Jesse. He knew just

how the willow tree felt. Jesse had once been in-fested with parasites when they lived in Costa Rica. The doctor there had prescribed a medicine that tasted like skunk soup with mouse turd dumplings.

"We're sorry about your troubles," said Daisy, not sounding sorry at all.

"We're going to try real hard to help you," said Jesse. "Won't we, Daze?"

"We'll get the pickax and free both you and the queen," said Daisy.

Instead of comforting the willow, this only gave rise to a fresh torrent of tears. "Oh, please don't take that pickax to me. I can see it now. I'm to be chopped to kindling, whittled to wood chips, ground to sawdust! Sacrificed to Her Royal Low-ness, the Queen of the Mud Puppies. Say hello to the Sacrificial Willow! That's me!" he wailed. "Alas, alas!"

"They aren't mud puppies," Daisy told him crossly. "They're hobgoblins, and they deserve our respect."

"Oh, really?" said the willow. "I don't see any-one respecting me!"

"We do," said Jesse. "Don't we, Daze?"

Not very convincingly, Daisy nodded.

After standing around listening to him carry on for a few more minutes, Jesse and Daisy pried themselves away. When they and the dryads were standing once more outside the willow's drooping canopy, Jesse said, "Well, he certainly lives up to his name."

Daisy said, "It's hard to feel sorry for someone who feels quite that sorry for himself."

"Th-th-thank you for taking the time to pay your r-r-r-respects all the same," said Lady Aspen. "Believe it or not, it meant a great deal to him."

"And to every one of us," said Douglas Fir.

With that, the two dryads went back beneath the canopy of willow leaves to be with their friend.

CHAPTER NINE

THE FERN BRIGADE

Jesse and Daisy were just entering the Deep Woods when Jesse noticed a stirring in the ferns growing near the base of the Douglas fir. Maybe it was just a chipmunk, but Jesse didn't want anything messing with the tree while its dryad wasn't in residence to defend it. "Hold up," he said to Daisy. "I need to check out those ferns."

Daisy nodded and stopped, but she wasn't paying much attention. Her mind was on their plan. It would be a long drop from the side of the ramp down to the ground of the cavern. What if they figured out a way to drop down *on top* of the big book? Perhaps the magical shield would break their fall. On the other hand, it might squeak and give them away. She looked over to Jesse to share these thoughts, but he was nowhere to be seen!

"Hey, Jess!" she called out, looking all around. "Where'd you go?"

"What do you mean?" he said.

He sounded close by, but Daisy couldn't see him. "Are you behind the Douglas fir?" she asked.

"I'm in front of it. In the ferns . . . in plain sight. Do you need glasses?" he asked.

"Maybe, because I'm looking right at the fir tree and I can't see you," Daisy said.

"Well, look a little harder," Jesse said, popping back into view as he walked toward Daisy.

Daisy said, "Whoa! Wait a sec, Jess." She held up her hand.

Jesse stopped.

"Back up to the ferns again," Daisy said.

This struck Jesse as a pretty strange request,

but he backed up. The ferns made a swishing sound around his ankles. He stood there and watched her face. There was a look of amazement on it.

"Jess, this is completely incredible!" she said, jumping up and down and flapping her hands. "I see the ferns moving, but I don't see you. You're invisible!"

"I'm *what*?" he asked.

"When you stand in the ferns, you're one hundred percent *invisible,*" she said. "Let's change places and see if it works for me."

Jesse stood where Daisy had been and Daisy went to take his place in the ferns. Jesse watched as his cousin simply slipped out of sight.

"Do you realize how great this is?" Daisy's voice said.

Jesse thought it was cool, but it was also kind of creepy. What was causing it?

"Come here, Jesse," said Daisy. "Help me choose a couple of nice, fat ferns. The bigger and bushier, the better."

Jesse hesitated and then joined Daisy in the fern bed. He still couldn't see her, but he heard her breathing right next to him. He asked her, "Why are we fern-picking?"

Daisy said, "Because ferns have magical properties, Jess. I read about it in one of my plant books, and you *proved* it." Before he could stop her, she had launched into one of her botanical lectures. "The fern is one of the most ancient plants on the earth. In medieval times, people thought the fern could make them invisible. The Green Man, a mythical character that dates back practically to cave days, covered his face with a mask of ferns to make himself invisible."

"So you're thinking that Emmy's hatching made the ferns magic again, like in olden days," said Jesse thoughtfully.

"Exactly!" said Daisy. "And the reason St. George hasn't sucked the magic out of them is 'cause they are growing in a safe place, beneath one of the two free trees."

"So Miss Alodie's protective spell is covering them," Jesse said.

"Exactly!" replied Daisy. "It makes complete sense when you think about it. These two look good. Let's step away from the fern patch and see what happens."

Jesse went back to the path, but he couldn't see Daisy. "Are you still in the fern patch?" he called out.

She laughed in his ear. "I'm right next to you! Funny, I don't *feel* invisible." The next moment, she was visible and two large ferns floated to the ground between them. "Can you see me now?" she asked.

"Wow!" Jesse said.

"As long as I hold the ferns, you can't see me," said Daisy.

"Cool," Jesse said. "My turn."

"Try it with just one fern," Daisy said.

Jesse bent and picked up a fern. He could tell by the look in Daisy's eyes that she could no longer see him. He sneaked around and stood behind Daisy, tapping her on the shoulder. She whirled to face him. He dropped the fern, grinning. "We can each hold a fern, sneak down into the cavern and steal the Golden Pickax. St. George won't know what hit him," said Jesse.

"That's what I call a *plan*!" said Daisy.

They did a quick happy prospector's dance before choosing two fresh ferns and continuing down the path toward the clearing in the Deep Woods.

On the way, Daisy noticed that Jesse kept getting in her way and jostling her. She kept stepping on his toe. "We're going to need to stay close together when we use these," she said as they walked.

"Of course," said Jesse.

"I mean, really close. We'll have to hold hands," said Daisy.

"Really?" said Jesse. "How come?"

"Because otherwise we won't know where the other one is," she said. "If we hold hands, at least we can *feel* each other's presence. Get it?"

"Of course!" said Jesse. He took Daisy's hand, just to practice. It felt funny, like being a little kid again. "We shouldn't talk or make any kind of noise, either," he said. "The ferns might make us invisible, but they won't hide our sound."

"Good thinking," said Daisy as they came to the edge of the clearing.

They stopped and stared. The clearing was empty. There were no St. George, no hobgoblins, no machinery. Not a single tool lay anywhere about. Even the high mountain of dirt had disappeared. For a minute, Jesse was afraid that St. George had gone and removed all traces of himself, as he had from the college. Then he saw a large, dark rectangular patch in the middle of the clearing. Jesse led Daisy toward it. With their invisible hands locked and their ferns held tight, Jesse and Daisy stood and looked down into the hole.

The wooden ramp they had walked up earlier that morning was still there. They both took big deep breaths and tiptoed down it into the under-ground cavern.

Halfway down the ramp, they stopped. They could see St. George. He was lounging on the hobgoblin queen's throne, holding the Golden Pickax. But it didn't look very golden. It looked crusted with dirt and rust. St. George was rubbing the pickax briskly with something that looked like a scrubbing brush. The Slayer paused and lifted the pickax to examine it. The very tip of one prong was now bright gold. St. George lowered the pickax and went to work again.

Jesse felt Daisy tugging him slowly but steadily backward, up the ramp and into the clearing, where she stopped and laid down her fern. He did the same. "Okay," she said. "So we didn't plan for him to be actually *holding* the pickax. I say we go back down, get up super-close to him, and the minute he lays down that pickax, *whammo*! We grab it and take off—"

"Through the tunnel to Her Royal Lowness," Jesse said. "But what if he doesn't take a break? Did you see that thing? It's filthy! He could be cleaning it for hours! And what if one of us burps or sneezes or something while we're waiting around? He's bound to hear us and then what?"

"Good point." Daisy went back to thinking.

"So you think we should . . . what? Just go down there and yank it away from him?" she said.

"I think if you can distract him, I can get it away from him," Jesse said.

Daisy was surprised. "Really?" she said.

Jesse said, "Yes!"

They quickly revised their plan. It wasn't completely satisfactory. They didn't know for a fact that the pickax would become invisible once it was in Jesse's possession, but they had to assume that it would. The pack on Jesse's back was as invisible as he was when the fern was in his hand, so it seemed possible. When they were finished planning, they nodded solemnly and picked up their ferns.

"All right, then," said Jesse. His heart was thudding. They were as ready as they were ever going to be. They reached out and found each other's hand, held tight to their ferns, and stole back down the ramp. They walked all the way down it and across the cavern to the hobgoblin queen's throne. They stopped about a foot away from St. George. Jesse recoiled from the man's rotting-meat breath, and his hand that held the fern trembled. The hand holding Daisy's was slick with sweat.

St. George went completely still for a moment. Then his nostrils started to twitch.

He can smell us, Jesse thought.

St. George slowly lowered the copper brush and looked first to the right and then to the left, his nostrils working all the while. The light flashed on the disks of his wireless glasses as his eyes came to rest directly on Jesse. Jesse stopped breathing—one second, two seconds, three seconds—as time seemed to stretch into eternity.

Finally, with a quick shake of his head, St. George went back to rubbing the Golden Pickax. Jesse started breathing again. He was bathed in sweat and a little dizzy from holding his breath, but it was now or never.

Jesse gave Daisy's hand a firm squeeze. Almost immediately, her hand slid out of his. Jesse had an impulse to reach out and grab it back. It suddenly felt all wrong to break contact with her, but it was too late to change their plan now.

Seconds later, St. George's head jerked backward. His hands fell away from the pickax as he sat up and swung around to see who had just given his hair such a pull. Jesse seized the pickax and muffled a cry. The pickax was *heavy*! He had to lift it one-handed because the other hand was holding the fern. With all his strength, he swung the pickax up onto his shoulder, like a hobgoblin.

St. George swung back around and gaped at his

empty lap. He leaped in the air and landed in a crouch, hissing, "Who's there?"

Jesse dodged out of St. George's reach as he lunged forward, moving this way and that, sweeping the air with his long arms. Jesse backed up toward a nearby torch-lit tunnel. He hoped it led to the queen's jail. The tunnels all looked alike, but this one felt right to him.

St. George pounced on the exact spot where Jesse had been standing a second before. With a petrified yelp, Jesse whipped around and ran. Almost instantly, he collided headlong with what felt like a wall.

Jesse sat down hard, arms flopping to his sides, his fern on the ground a foot away. For a moment he saw stars. When the stars faded, he saw Daisy, also fully visible, sitting opposite him with her legs splayed out, rubbing her nose. The Golden Pickax lay beside him.

"I knew it was a mistake to stop holding hands," Daisy muttered.

"One hopes it will be your last," St. George said, strolling over to them. He leaned down and picked up the fallen ferns. He tore them to shreds and scattered the pieces, smirking.

Daisy scowled up at him. "What's so funny?" she said.

"Why, you are, of course!" he said.

"What are you going to do with us?" Daisy asked.

"What else, you silly little fool? I'll use you to bait my hook and go dragon-fishing. And I'm sure to land me a fine catch, with such perfect *worms* for bait."

Daisy sneered at St. George. "Emmy's too smart to go for your bait. You're going to need a cleverer plan than that," she said.

St. George swooped down and brought his face to within inches of hers. The blast of foul breath made her turn her head to the side and hold her nose.

"Oh, she'll go for it," said St. George. "That nub-tailed little canine of yours is going to come running to your rescue."

Jesse maintained an even expression as he said, "What's our dog got to do with any of this?"

St. George drew himself up. "Oh, you two think you're quite the little wizards, don't you? But the laurel dryads told me all about how she transforms into a dragon as she passes under their gossip-happy noses, day in and day out. Don't you know that I have far too many spies in this world for you to be able to keep anything from me?" He dusted off his hands. "And now, dear ones, I have precious little time for chitchat."

"And what makes you think we would ever want to chat with a rat like you?" Jesse said. As he said this, he nudged Daisy's leg with his foot and raised one eyebrow in the direction of the ramp. She raised an eyebrow in response and nodded her head slightly.

"RUN!" screamed Jesse.

Daisy and Jesse both leaped to their feet and took off, but St. George clamped a hand on the backs of their necks and held them in place.

"Really?" St. George said. "Leaving so fast? I wouldn't hear of it!"

As if they were no heavier than a couple of parcels, he gathered them both up in one arm and grasped the Golden Pickax with the other. He carried all three over to the big book and dumped them beside it. Then he began to work his way around them and the book in a wide circle. The cousins actually heard the invisible membrane squeak as St. George stretched it this way and that.

"There," he said, sealing it with a final wave of his hand. "That ought to keep you out of mischief. Don't bother trying to break through. You'll only exhaust yourselves. Why not use some of that youthful energy and finish polishing the rust off the Golden Pickax? I'm off to town. With any luck, when I return, I'll find a dragon in my trap." He chuckled as he marched up the ramp and out of the chamber.

The moment he was gone, Jesse took off the backpack. "Here's the jar of worms," he said, pulling it out.

"Quick," said Daisy, "before he comes back!"

Jesse unscrewed the lid, knelt down, and gently emptied the contents of the jar. Six pink earthworms wriggled wildly about on the ground.

"What's happening?" said Jesse, standing back.

"They're getting bigger, I think," said Daisy, giving them a wide berth. "Definitely, a lot bigger!"

In minutes, the worms became as thick and long as the foam noodles people use in swimming pools—only the worms' skins were glistening and pink like chewed bubblegum. Then the worms lined up, side by side, and started burrowing into the ground beneath the invisible wall. Jesse and Daisy watched, goggle-eyed, as the giant earthworms dug a deep trench big enough for the cousins to crawl out to escape their invisible prison. Daisy went through first, then Jesse, dragging the pickax behind him.

The worms, back to their normal size, were crawling away, each in its own direction.

"I guess they've earned their freedom," Daisy said wistfully.

"Hey, guys, hold up!" Jesse called out to them, but the worms paid him no mind. He said to Daisy, "Too bad they couldn't hang around long enough to get the book for us. Miss Alodie won't like that we used her worms but didn't get the book."

"We can't help that," Daisy said with an impatient sweep of her arms. "We're doing the best we can, aren't we? Jeesh!"

"Right, so let's get this pickax to Her Royal Lowness and let the revolution begin!" Jesse said.

"Time to turn the tide of battle," Daisy agreed.

"Jesse! Daisy! Is that you?" Emmy's golden voice rang out to them from above.

"How did she get out?" Daisy whispered frantically.

"We're down here, Em!" Jesse called up, then gave Daisy a look of panic. "What'll we do? She's walking right into the trap!"

"Don't come down!" Daisy called up to Emmy. "We'll come up to you." She whispered furiously to Jesse, "Remember what the professor said? We need to keep her out of the way. You bring the pickax to the queen. I'll take Emmy back to the lair.

I mean, the garage. I'll meet you back at the barn. Good luck, Jess."

"But I have to come," said Emmy, who was already halfway down the ramp.

Jesse and Daisy ran to meet her. Emmy's great green eyes were pooled with tears.

"How did you get out of the garage?" Jesse asked her gently.

"My friends let me out," Emmy said in a small voice.

"Like they did before?" Daisy asked, caressing the smooth scales on Emmy's back.

Emmy nodded, sniffling. "They said I had to go to St. George and lay my life at his feet. So here I am." She lifted her face to the patch of blue sky visible through the hole overhead and let out a long, plaintive wail. Then she took in a deep sucking breath and fell to weeping as if her heart would break.

Daisy wished she hadn't given away her bandanna. This was turning out to be a very teary day! She dabbed at Emmy's tears with the bottom of her extra-long T-shirt.

After a final burbling honk of dragon tears and snot into Daisy's shirt, Emmy said with a stamp of her hind leg, "I *like* my life. I don't *want* to lay it at St. George's stinky feet. Douglas Fir and Lady

Aspen are *mean* friends! I don't like them anymore."

Daisy and Jesse exchanged worried looks.

"Why would the dryads say a thing like that to Emmy?" Jesse wondered.

"Why would they want to sacrifice her like that?" Daisy said.

"Because I commanded them to," St. George said, sauntering down the ramp. Dangling from his bony fingers were two long tattered strips of gaily colored fabric.

The last two trees had fallen.

143

CHAPTER TEN

THE WILLOW SONG

At first, every scale on Emmy's body stood up like small razor blades. Then her form grew fuzzy and started to change in slow motion. It was as if her ability to mask had not only grown sluggish but uncertain as well, as if she weren't quite sure what to mask herself as. First she became a rhinoceros, then a lion, then a shark with a whipping tail. These images morphed into each other and overlapped so that one moment she was a shark with a rhino horn and the next, a lion with a dorsal fin. It was painful for the cousins to watch, but St. George found it all very entertaining.

"Oh, dear. Some days it's so *difficult* to decide what to put on, isn't it? I think I have the perfect thing for you," he said with a brisk clap of his hands. The ringing nearby ceased and a gang of hobgoblins trooped out from one of the tunnels into the cavern, dragging a long and heavy length of iron chain with them.

"Bind her," St. George said, pointing to Emmy, who, having failed to find a satisfying form, had changed back to her dragon self.

Obediently, the hobgoblins wrapped the chain around and around Emmy.

"You," said the Slayer, pointing to Jesse. "Bring me the Golden Pickax."

"Don't do it, Jess!" Daisy told him. "You're not his slave!"

Jesse didn't want to do it, but his body ached to. He cast a helpless look over his shoulder at her as, against his will, he crawled beneath the invisible wall and brought the Golden Pickax back to

St. George, offering it up with shaking arms.

"Jess, what are you doing?" Daisy cried out.

"I can't help it, Daze. It's like my body is obeying him even though my mind wants to run and butt him in the belly."

"Well, I don't have to obey him," said Daisy fiercely. But when she went to take the Golden Pickax away from Jesse, she found that she couldn't move. She was in a prison no larger than the skin of her own body. It was worse than being stuck behind the bathtub!

"Jesse!" she cried, panic gripping her. "I can't move!"

"Stay calm," said Jesse. "Take deep breaths." Jesse tried to take his own advice as he held the pickax out to the Dragon Slayer, the muscles in his arms quivering with the strain.

"Stand there and hold it," said St. George. He waved his arms and brought the invisible wall down with a loud squeak. Then he clapped his hands and the squad of hobgoblins reassembled before him, ready to receive their next order.

"Fill in that trench!" he commanded, pointing to the hole the giant earthworms had dug.

The hobgoblins formed a line. Digging with their shovels in unison, they quickly filled the hole.

When they were finished, they stood at attention and waited.

"Wheel the cart over to the dragon," St. George ordered, pointing to where Emmy stood in chains, her head hanging. Enormous dragon tears dropped off her snout and plopped onto the dirt at her feet.

A thick rope hung from the coupling on the front of the wagon. The hobgoblins picked it up. Bending forward as one and with a mighty grunting heave-ho, they began to haul the cart over to Emmy.

St. George unbuttoned his long black coat. Jesse and Daisy both gasped. Beneath the coat, he wore heavy silver hose and a white doublet embroidered with the bright red coat of arms of Saint George the Dragon Slayer. On his Web site, the professor had shown the cousins pictures of Saint George as he had been depicted in so many paintings and stained glass windows. And now here he was, in the flesh. He wasn't saintly at all!

St. George stood before the big book. For a moment, he closed his eyes and bowed his head. Then he opened his eyes and jabbed his hands at the book. A yellowish-greenish-brownish light shot out from his fingertips. The light didn't just *look* sickening. It actually made both Jesse and Daisy want to throw up. With a loud creak and a flapping of pages, the cover of the big book lifted, like a drawbridge rising. The book fell open to a place in the middle.

Jesse got a whiff of must and mildew and red-hot chili peppers. He found that the familiar smell calmed his stomach.

St. George clapped his hands again. "Light!" he called to the two hobgoblins sprawled in the dirt at his feet. Daisy noticed that whenever they weren't busy, the hobgoblins sank to the ground and moaned and wept pitiful mud tears.

The hobgoblins stopped swaying and weeping and jumped to their wedgelike feet. Then they scuttled off into one of the tunnels, returning momentarily with two flaming torches. They stood a little behind and to either side of St. George as he leaned over the book, the torchlight dancing on the lenses of his glasses. He ran a finger down the page and moved his lips silently.

Jesse's muscles burned beneath the weight of the pickax, still in his hands, his arms trembling. He caught a glimpse of black symbols marching down a creamy page of brightly painted pictures of dragons with their blood spilling everywhere. He swallowed, hoping against hope that he wasn't about to be ordered to take part in the slaying of his own beloved Emerald.

Emmy had gone still and silent beneath her shroud of chains. Her eyes were dull, and her lustrous blue-green scales had turned a milky gray. Daisy stared at Emmy, her face twisting in misery while the rest of her stayed frozen.

St. George muttered something. Then he looked up from the book, held out both arms, and said, "The pickax. Give it to me. *Now, boy!*"

Jesse, fighting his body every inch of the way, offered the pickax to the Dragon Slayer.

St. George took the pickax from him and held it up in both hands, lifting it high over the open book. His entire body started to tremble. Beads of sweat broke out on his pale brow. Then he walked over to Emmy. *Whoosh!* He swung the pickax high above his head. Emmy cringed and squeezed her eyes shut. The torchlight glinted on the one golden prong of the pickax as it came down on the dragon. Jesse and Daisy both cried out.

But the pickax froze inches from Emmy's body. St. George's initial look of irritation quickly turned to fear as the pickax exploded into flames.

Emmy lifted her head. Her eyes, reflecting the flames, shone brightly as she watched the fire burn.

Then she said, "Make a wish!" and blew out the fire with a mighty breath.

The hobgoblins let out a collective sigh of satisfaction. "Ahhhhhhh!"

From its handle to its two sharp prongs, the pickax had turned to dazzling solid gold.

St. George grunted as the now truly golden pickax dragged him backward, away from Emmy, and over to a mound of rocks in the corner. There the pickax arced high in the air and came down hard on a large rock. As it struck the stone, a deafening sound like a gong rang out and echoed through the chamber.

St. George let out an agonized *"Nooooooooo!"*

Again the pickax swung back and this time came down on a smaller rock. A higher note sounded. The pickax swung back and came down on a third rock, and a fourth, and a fifth, and on and on, as the melody built and swelled and filled the underground cavern. Whether St. George liked it or not, the pickax was picking out a tune, playing this pile of ordinary, dusty rocks as if they were some sort of crazy natural xylophone. The song it played was haunting and sad and heartbreakingly beautiful.

The hobgoblins stirred and sat up, listening to the music and wagging their heads, some of them even beginning to hum along. Emmy's body, beneath the chains, swayed. "It's the willow song," she said with pride. "I love it!"

The next moment, a great hoarse bellow echoed down the tunnel. "We're coming, rough gems of the earth! We're coming, you darling little axey-waxey, you! We're on our way! Mummy's back!"

The next instant, Her Royal Lowness herself, Queen Hap of the Hobgoblin Hive of Hobhorn, came crashing into the chamber, robe held high above her regal bowlegged knees.

The hobgoblins scrambled down onto their knees and touched their foreheads to the ground.

Jesse ran over to Daisy. "The Golden Pickax freed the queen!" he cried.

Daisy took a tentative step toward Jesse and cried out, "Me too!"

"What about me three?" said Emmy in a small voice.

Daisy and Jesse ran to the dragon and tried to pull the chain off her, but it was too heavy.

"How come the Golden Pickax didn't free Emmy, too?" Daisy asked.

"St. George probably put a superstrong spell on the chain," said Jesse.

"Did not!" Emmy said with a pout. "It's because

it's stinky old iron! Dragons *hate* iron. It stinks!"

"I'm sorry, Em," said Daisy, touching her gently through the chain, "but don't worry. We'll get it off you as fast as we can."

"Maybe Her Royal Lowness can help," said Jesse, waving to get the queen's attention. But her moss-green eyes were scanning the cavern.

"There it is! Mummy's pet!" the queen cried, lighting on the pickax. Running over to a cringing St. George, she yanked the Golden Pickax from his lifeless grip.

Just then, the cavern filled with a rhythmic *hut-hut-hut* like the steady beat of marching feet. Seconds later, seven hobgoblins strutted proudly into view from the nearby tunnel.

"It's the faithful band of rebels!" Daisy exclaimed happily.

Gone were the orange jumpsuits. The hobgoblins now wore stout plates of armor and bore all manner of medieval weaponry: pikes and halberds, lances and flails, and maces and morning stars, bristling with angry spikes.

"We'll take it from here, Georgie Porgie!" the queen said to the cowering Slayer. Her Royal Lowness hefted the Golden Pickax to play the rocks. As the music swelled, it began to take on an uptempo beat. More and more armed hobgoblins poured forth from the other tunnels, all armored and carrying weaponry. Between the music of the Golden Pickax and the darkly muttering hobgoblin horde, the cavern was thrumming with noise and excitement.

With a final, crashing chord, the queen lowered the pickax. A hush fell over the cavern. As the last note of music faded, Her Royal Lowness went over to Emmy and got down on both knees. She reverently placed the Golden Pickax before her and touched her forehead to the ground.

"Awwwwww!" The hobgoblins sighed happily to one another.

Rising, Her Royal Lowness said to Jesse and Daisy, "Stand aside, Upper Realmers!"

The cousins obeyed, backing away from Emmy.

Then the hobgoblin queen placed one tip of the Golden Pickax to the chain. Like a lit fuse, a flame traveled along the chain and, link by link, sizzled it to white ash in seconds.

Emmy rose up and shook the ashes from her scales. "Thank you, Queenie-weenie!" she said.

"We are honored to serve!" said the queen. Then she spat on the tip of the pickax and polished it on the sleeve of her robe. "Ah, we make a fine team, together with our axey-waxey, do we not?" she said with a happy grin.

The hobgoblins erupted into a cheer that settled into a chant: "Hob! Gob! Hob! Gob! Hobbledy-gobbledy-hob-gob-gob!" as hundreds of hobgoblin heads bobbed along with their weapons.

"I have a feeling the tide just officially turned," Daisy said to Jesse.

Jesse frowned. In the hubbub he had lost sight of St. George. "Wait a minute!" Then he cupped his hands to his mouth and shouted, "Where is the Slayer!"

The hobgoblins stopped chanting and looked around, snuffling and muttering among themselves.

"I see him! I see him! I see the bad man! Over there!" Emmy shouted, bouncing up and down and pointing.

Daisy caught a glimpse of red and white underneath the ramp. "He's beneath the ramp!" she called out.

"Seize him!" shouted the queen.

Growling, the hobgoblins rushed at St. George, brandishing their weapons and chanting, "Hob! Gob! Hob! Gob!" as they swarmed over him. But St. George picked them up and plucked them off him like so many burrs. Then he scrambled onto the ramp and ran to the top. There he raised his arms over his head and brought forth more of the same stomach-wrenching light from his fingertips. An avalanche of rocks came crashing down around him, blocking the way out.

The hobgoblins howled in outrage.

"Oh, no! We're trapped again!" Jesse cried out.

"Don't fret, lambies!" yelled the queen. "You can't trap a hobgoblin underground. There are other ways out of here. Follow us."

"But we can't leave without the book!" Jesse yelled.

Yet another wave of that foul light flashed. This time rocks showered down and buried the big book in a mountain of rubble.

Daisy swallowed her nausea and waved away the dust. "*Now* what?" she asked.

"Hobbies!" shouted the queen. "Smite the Slayer and make him squeal!"

The hobgoblins let out a rock-rumbling roar. From where Jesse and Daisy were standing, they had a clear view of the hobgoblins as they rushed up the ramp toward the Slayer. St. George pulled out a broad sword from a sheath on his hip. Its jeweled hilt sparkled in the torchlight. St. George set to slashing at the hobgoblins as if they were a field of overgrown weeds.

"Poor hobbies!" said Daisy, turning away.

"Nonsense!" boomed Her Royal Lowness. "Hobbies love a good *clash*! Let's leave them to it.

You and the draggy-wagon, come with us!"

"But the book!" Jesse and Daisy cried.

"The book? The book? Is that all you Upper Realmers care about, some book? Can't you see that our stalwart hobbies have their hands full at the present?" Queen Hap croaked.

It looked, indeed, as if every last hobgoblin were needed to bring down St. George.

"But we can't leave it buried here!" Daisy shouted over the din.

"We *promised*!" Jesse said.

"Leave it you must," bellowed the queen.

That was when Emmy stepped forward and said, "I think I can! I think I can!"

Suddenly Emmy's irises began to spin like a set of brilliant green pinwheels. Her nostrils gave off three puffs of peppery pinkish smoke, which rose up and radiated outward, filling the cavern with a bright, hot, pulsing light. The very next instant, the rocks and rubble rose up into the air and moved off to the side as if an invisible hand were rearranging them. In seconds, the book was completely uncovered.

One of the hobgoblins broke from the rear ranks and ran over to the book. He climbed on top of it and dusted it off with Daisy's bandanna.

"I knew I could!" Emmy said proudly. "Levitating spell. I just deuced it."

"Aced it," Jesse corrected.

"Emmy, that was *brilliant!*" said Daisy.

Emmy looked modest. "I am a very practical dragon sometimes! Climb up on the big book, Jesse and Daisy. We need to get out now. Climb on, please, welcome aboard, and thank you for flying the big book."

"You want us to climb on top of the book?" Jesse shouted.

"And the book's gonna fly?" Daisy added.

Emmy nodded vigorously. "Quickly, now, please, thank you. Her Royal Lowness is waiting."

The queen was tapping her big wedge of a foot impatiently. The hobgoblin with the purple bandanna hopped off the book and gestured wildly at the battle. The fray had worked its way down from the ramp and was swarming across the cavern toward them. The hobgoblin knelt before them and made a stirrup of his hands.

"We have no time to lose, lambies!" said the queen.

"What about St. George?" Jesse asked.

St. George's sword slashed in all directions, raising sparks as it struck against hobgoblin armor.

He seemed to be holding his own as he headed toward them.

"Don't give it another thought," said the queen, grinning like a jack-o'-lantern. "Our hobbies are just playing with him."

Jesse and Daisy let the hobgoblin boost them onto the book.

The next instant, the book rose up and hovered in the air. "We're floating!" said Jesse.

"Hang on!" said Emmy.

"Follow us," said the queen, heading for one of the old mine tunnels.

The book moved forward and Jesse and Daisy nearly tumbled off it.

"Don't worry," said Emmy. "I will run behind you and catch you if you fall."

The cousins grabbed hold of each other as the book scooted forward. It stopped, then started and stopped, as if it were testing its brakes. Finally, it zipped over to the tunnel and dipped slightly, like a raft joining the current of a stream.

The queen jogged just ahead of them. She held her robes high above her knees while her torch-bearing attendant kept pace with her. Emmy brought up the rear, casting an occasional glance over her shoulder toward the cavern. Gradually, the din of the battle began to fade behind them and was replaced by the soft *whooshing* of the big book as it wove through the tunnels that made up the vast underground maze of the Lower Realm.

At last, they came to a dead end. A soft golden-blue light shone from above. Jesse and Daisy looked up and saw a thicket of bushes stirring above them in a gentle breeze. Compared to the inferno they had left behind, the scene above was peaceful and quiet.

"This way out!" said the queen with a single upward stab of her hand. "Mind the prickers on those berry bushes."

"Will you be going back?" Daisy asked the queen.

"Of course we will!" she said. "Can't leave all the fun to our hobbies, can we?"

"Watch out for St. George," Jesse said. "He's a very dirty fighter."

"Nobody fights as dirty as a hobgoblin," she said with a roguish glint in her magnificent moss-green eyes.

"What will you do with him after you've defeated him?" asked Daisy.

"Trap him," growled the queen, "like a bug in amber."

"Will your hobbies be all right?" Jesse asked.

"They will be fine. I'm about to toss in a little

shake-up, Queen Hap–style," she said with a wink.

"Good-bye, Your Lowness," said Jesse. "And thanks for helping us."

"Thank *you* for finding our Golden Pickax," she said. "Good-bye, draggy-wagon, and good-bye, Keepers. We have no doubt we will be seeing you again in the Lower Realm someday . . . when the time is right."

"Thank you, you're welcome, come again soon, don't forget to write!" said Emmy.

Their last glimpse of the Lower Realm was of the queen's hobgoblin escort waving a wistful farewell to them with the purple bandanna.

The next minute, the book whisked them out of the hole. Pricker bushes snagged their clothing as they surged upward into the fresh air. Emmy climbed out after them, stopping to grab a handful of berries to cram into her bright pink mouth.

Aboveground, darkness had begun to fall. The Deep Woods throbbed with the reassuringly friendly sound of peepers.

Jesse looked at his watch. It was 8:20 in the evening. "Time sure flies in the Lower Realm," he said.

"Books do, too," Daisy couldn't resist adding.

Reluctantly tearing herself away from the fat, ripe berries, Emmy ran to catch up with the book as it bore the cousins through the Deep Woods. The trees leaned to either side to make way for them, and it wasn't long before they broke out of the woods and into the pasture.

"I think I'm going to call it the Hobhorn from now on," said Daisy, with a backward glance at the mountain previously known as Old Mother. The waterfall was swollen from the recent rains and it gushed down the rock face like molten silver beneath the rising moon. "And she's crying buckets, just like a real live hobgoblin. Only a little less muddy!"

But Jesse wasn't looking at the Hobhorn. He was looking at the pasture before them. "Wow!" he said. "Look, Daze!"

Daisy turned to see. "Holy moly," she said.

Stretched out across the pasture, from barn to brook, from the Deep Woods to the laurel bushes, was a vast circle of translucent dryads, of all shapes and sizes. Their long arms were intertwined as they moved together across the clover in a slow, rhythmic dance.

"There must be hundreds of them!" Jesse exclaimed.

"Thousands," said Daisy.

"It's the Great Dance of the Dryads!" Emmy said in a hushed voice.

Two figures broke away from the dance and approached them.

"Well done, Emerald. And well done, Dragon Keepers!" said Douglas Fir.

"We are dancing to c-c-c-celebrate our l-l-l-liberation from St. G-G-George's spell," said Lady Aspen.

A third figure came up behind them. He was thin and wrinkly, with a head of long straggly green hair and eyes that had huge green bags slung beneath them. Jesse and Daisy would have known the dryad anywhere.

"I think someone wants to thank you," said Douglas Fir, stepping aside. "Willow?"

"*Thank* them!" said the willow. "I want to fall to the earth and kiss their feet! Oh, I am so happy to be free of my recent . . . unpleasantness. You have no idea! Why, I'm so happy . . . I could cry!"

"Please don't," said Daisy through a fixed smile.

"We're glad we could help," said Jesse, although he wasn't sure how much help they had actually been. "Really, it was the hobgoblins—" He stopped and clutched at Daisy's arm. A faint rumbling noise sounded from somewhere nearby under the earth. "What's that?" he asked uneasily.

The dryads stopped dancing and cocked their leafy heads, listening.

"That would be Her Lowness," said Douglas Fir. "She's giving the earth a little shake-up, Queen Hap–style."

"Do you mean an earthquake?" Daisy asked.

Douglas Fir nodded. "Yes. A small one. Very concentrated."

"D-d-d-do not worry," said the aspen. "It's a v-v-v-very g-g-g-g-good sign!"

"St. George has been defeated," Douglas Fir stated.

"I sure hope so," said Jesse.

The next minute, the earth stopped rumbling and the dryads took up their dance again.

"Can you stay and join the dance?" asked the willow. "I promise I'll stay as dry as a Texas cotton-wood in a drought."

"You'll be our very special guests," Douglas Fir promised.

"W-w-w-we would be honored to have you in our midst," said Lady Aspen.

"Thanks," said Daisy, "but we can't tonight. I promised my mother we'd get to bed early. It's been a very long couple of days."

"And nights!" said Emmy.

"But we can't go home yet," said Jesse. "First we need to drop off the big book at Miss Alodie's house."

"I have a feeling she'll be waiting for us," said Daisy.

"Well, if you're leaving the Dell with that thing," said Douglas Fir, "you'll be needing some of these." He held out a fistful of ferns.

CHAPTER ELEVEN

THE PERFECT COFFEE TABLE BOOK

Although Jesse, Daisy, and Emmy all held their ferns tightly, they didn't fool Miss Alodie one bit. She saw them plain as day as she stood in her backyard, her garden doors flung wide open. Waving her arms like a member of an airport ground crew, she guided the book through the open doors to land softly in the middle of her parlor.

"Heigh-ho, cousins, I've been expecting you!" said Miss Alodie, laughing merrily as she followed them inside and closed the garden doors firmly behind her.

Jesse and Daisy tumbled off the book, rolling into a heap on the soft rug. For a few minutes, they just lay there on the floor, side by side, safe and sound, and visible once again.

Eventually, they both sat up and looked around. It was the first time either of them had ever been inside Miss Alodie's house. The inside of her house looked a lot like the outside. There were flowers everywhere: flowers in the wallpaper, flowers on the furniture covers, on the little throw pillows, on the rug, and even on the lamp shades! The air smelled of flowers, too, and it wasn't the kind of fragrance that comes from a spray or one of those scented candles. It was the smell of real live flowers, all mingled together into one giant heady bouquet.

Not surprisingly, Daisy exclaimed, "I love your house!"

"Why, thank you, Daisy Flower." Miss Alodie

lifted a floral tablecloth and put it over the big book, which had settled itself between the chintz couch and a pair of chintz-covered armchairs. Their hostess bustled around, making a careful arrangement on top of the cloth: a fan of gardening magazines, a flower-topped candy box, and a flowered vase with flowers in it. In no time at all, the book looked right at home.

Miss Alodie stood back and admired her work with a happy sigh. "I've always wanted to have an honest-to-goodness coffee table book, and now I have one, thanks to you three. Would anyone care for tea? I have fairy cakes with lavender icing and an apricot ginger tisane."

Strange food, Jesse thought. But this time he was too hungry to refuse.

"That sounds great! But then we have to get home. I promised my mom," Daisy said through a king-size yawn.

Miss Alodie bustled over to the cozy little kitchen.

"Where's Emmy?" Jesse looked around in a sudden panic. Then he breathed a sigh of relief. She was fast asleep on the rug before the fireplace, in her sheepdog shape. Jesse laughed and pointed at her.

"She's completely pooped," said Daisy.

Miss Alodie carried in the tea tray. She wanted to hear all about their adventure. Between bites of cake (eaten off delicate plates decorated with a pattern of violets and vine leaves) and sips of perfume-tasting tisane (brewed from wildflowers and drunk from teacups shaped like tulips), the cousins filled her in on every last thrilling detail.

"So what's this dragon treasure that's not really a treasure?" Jesse asked.

"You'll find out all about it," said Miss Alodie.

"But when?" said Jesse.

"Don't tell us, we know," said Daisy.

"When the time is right," the cousins said together.

"How did you guess?" said Miss Alodie merrily.

"Meanwhile, what about the book?" asked Jesse. "We're dying to find out what's inside it. Can you read it to us?"

"Please?" Daisy begged.

"It will be my pleasure," said Miss Alodie with a twinkle in her eye. "As soon as I figure out how to myself!"

Over by the fireplace, Emmy woofed in her sleep, her furry legs running as fast as they could carry her up and away into her dragon dreams.

That night Jesse e-mailed his parents:

Dear Mom and Dad, The rain stopped and
Daisy and I finally got to go outside. We went
searching for treasure and hiked in the Deep
Woods and guess what else? We had an
earthquake! 6.9 on the Richter scale, the
local weather guy said. We're all fine except
that Mrs. Nosy-Britches' chimney got a big
crack in it. Ha! Don't worry; the quake was
nothing like the one that time in Pakistan.
This one was just a little shake-up. Anyway,
we've decided to take it easy for a while.
Hang out with Emmy (she's learning lots of
nifty new tricks) and catch up on some
summer reading. There's this great new
book we found. It's got a lot of pages and we
just can't wait to read it.
Love, your son in America, Jesse Tiger

Don't miss the Dragon Keepers' next adventure in
The Dragon in the Library!